Jet Set Docs

How far will they go to find the one they love?

Introducing this season's hottest Harlequin Medical Romance novels packed with your summertime dose of dreamy doctors, pulse-racing drama and sizzling romantic tension! Fly up, up and away and follow these globe-trotting docs as they travel to stunning international destinations for work…but end up finding a special someone in their arms!

Grab your passport and find out in

Second Chance in Santiago by Tina Beckett
One Night to Sydney Wedding by JC Harroway
The Doctor's Italian Escape by Annie Claydon
Spanish Doc to Heal Her by Karin Baine
ER Doc's South Pole Reunion by Juliette Hyland
Their Accidental Vegas Vows by Amy Ruttan

All available now!

Dear Reader,

Thank you for picking up a copy of Grace and Jonah's story, *Their Accidental Vegas Vows*.

I was so excited to write another book set in Vegas and especially to do one with an accidental wedding. Those are always fun and it was nice to have fun with this couple.

Grace has a lot of my traits, a bit anxious, definitely a people pleaser, but she really does love her family deep down. She's strong, though, and loves her job. She just has to work through her belief that she doesn't deserve love.

Jonah is a hero and he's been burned in love. His plan wasn't to make friends in Vegas, but that all changes after one night out with his partner, Grace.

Now they're pretending to be married, fighting their attraction and working together. Who knew that one mistake could lead to a lifetime of happiness?

I hope you enjoy Grace and Jonah's story!

I love hearing from readers, so please drop by my website, www.amyruttan.com.

With warmest wishes,

Amy Ruttan

THEIR ACCIDENTAL VEGAS VOWS

AMY RUTTAN

MEDICAL ROMANCE

If you purchased this book without a cover you should be aware that this book is stolen property. It was reported as "unsold and destroyed" to the publisher, and neither the author nor the publisher has received any payment for this "stripped book."

MEDICAL ROMANCE

ISBN-13: 978-1-335-94313-2

Their Accidental Vegas Vows

Copyright © 2025 by Amy Ruttan

All rights reserved. No part of this book may be used or reproduced in any manner whatsoever without written permission.

Without limiting the author's and publisher's exclusive rights, any unauthorized use of this publication to train generative artificial intelligence (AI) technologies is expressly prohibited.

This is a work of fiction. Names, characters, places and incidents are either the product of the author's imagination or are used fictitiously. Any resemblance to actual persons, living or dead, businesses, companies, events or locales is entirely coincidental.

For questions and comments about the quality of this book, please contact us at CustomerService@Harlequin.com.

TM and ® are trademarks of Harlequin Enterprises ULC.

 Harlequin Enterprises ULC
22 Adelaide St. West, 41st Floor
Toronto, Ontario M5H 4E3, Canada
www.Harlequin.com

Printed in U.S.A.

Born and raised just outside Toronto, Ontario, **Amy Ruttan** fled the big city to settle down with the country boy of her dreams. After the birth of her second child, Amy was lucky enough to realize her lifelong dream of becoming a romance author. When she's not furiously typing away at her computer, she's mom to three wonderful children, who use her as a personal taxi and chef.

Books by Amy Ruttan

Harlequin Medical Romance

Caribbean Island Hospital

Reunited with Her Surgeon Boss
A Ring for His Pregnant Midwife

Portland Midwives

The Doctor She Should Resist

Falling for the Billionaire Doc
Falling for His Runaway Nurse
Paramedic's One-Night Baby Bombshell
Winning the Neonatal Doc's Heart
Nurse's Pregnancy Surprise
Reunited with Her Off-Limits Surgeon
Tempted by the Single Dad Next Door
Rebel Doctor's Boston Reunion

Visit the Author Profile page
at Harlequin.com for more titles.

This book is for all the amazing authors I got to hang with at the Harlequin 75th and for my family who were very patient with me up north while I finished this book. Also, special shout-out to the bear who passed by our campsite—quite the shock to finish a book and see him walk by on his way to eat flowers.

Praise for
Amy Ruttan

"*Baby Bombshell for the Doctor Prince* is an emotional swoon-worthy romance.... Author Amy Ruttan beautifully brought these two characters together making them move towards their happy ever after. Highly recommended for all readers of romance."
—*Goodreads*

CHAPTER ONE

BREATHE. JUST BREATHE.

Grace was trying to take deep, even breaths to calm the rush of adrenaline coursing through her that was now mixed with a healthy dose of anxiety. That adrenaline was something she chased as a paramedic, especially in Las Vegas. She liked the high. It fueled her during the toughest times, but there were some cases that just got to her and there was no holding back the flood of emotions. No matter how hard she tried. And tonight had been one of them.

She closed her eyes and leaned back against the brick wall of the hospital in the ambulance bay and tried to remind herself that there was nothing to be upset or worried about. The child was going to be okay, but every time they pulled someone out of a pool or a hot tub from a near drowning it always got to her after.

Every. Single. Time.

What she wouldn't give to lie on the ground, her butt against the wall and her legs straight up in the air. It was a proven method to ease anxiety, and she did it often, at home. Really not something she could do here outside a hospital by the trauma room doors. It was also something she didn't want her colleagues to see. She worked hard to control her fear, her anxiety.

No one else needed to know about it.

"Hey, Landon. You okay?"

Grace groaned inwardly at being caught.

She opened her eyes and glanced up at her partner. They'd been paired up for the last six months, but every time she saw Jonah her stomach always did that nervous little flip because he was so easy on the eyes: tall, muscular, with a chiseled jaw and a small cleft in his chin, blue eyes, blond hair and the quintessential golden California tan. Fitting, since that was where he was from. He had told Grace so during their first meeting, after he'd told her to hang ten, which hadn't even made any sense at the time, and she had jokingly called him a surfer dude.

Jonah was exactly the type of guy she was attracted to, but as her partner he was off-limits. Grace was not going to make that same mistake twice. There was no way she was ever getting involved with someone she worked with or in close proximity to again.

She'd been there, done that and was still paying the price for it. It was hard to put the mistake of an ex behind you when he was one—a trauma doctor and you saw him on a regular basis because you were a paramedic, and two—the best friend of your little sister's fiancé and so was going to be at every single wedding event for the next month.

So no matter how attractive she found her partner Jonah, how tempting, he was completely off-limits. She was never going to mix business with pleasure again.

Even though sex would be a great way to relieve her current anxiety.

What is wrong with me?

Grace swallowed the lump in her throat and plastered a fake smile on her face. "Perfectly."

Jonah's eyes narrowed, and he smirked. "I don't buy it."

"What do you mean you don't buy it?"

"First, I'm older and wiser than you, and second, I served in the Marines. I know when I'm seeing a trauma response in someone."

Grace sighed and hugged her arms. "I guess you were bound to see it. It's drownings. They're difficult for me."

"But the little girl is going to be okay."

And it was this kind of response which made her reluctant to share with anyone her emotions. She'd learned to mask it well, even if it sometimes slipped, like now.

She nodded quickly, forcing a bright smile. "Oh, I know, but...it's hard."

Jonah didn't pry her with more questions. He

just nodded. "Well, let's get this rig back, and then I think we need to go out and have a drink."

"What?" she asked, surprised. Since Jonah had arrived, she'd never really seen him socialize with others. He was friendly enough but kept to himself. Just like she tended to do. Socializing at work was fine, but she liked to keep people at a distance ever since that disastrous workplace relationship.

"We're both off duty, and you look like you could use a drink. We'll get a group together and hit the Strip. What do you say?"

I should say no.

Only he wasn't wrong. She could really use a night out, and it would be nice to let off steam with some coworkers. She'd used to have fun with them, before her ex. If she went out maybe then she could release this last bit of anxious energy. She couldn't remember the last time she had let loose out on the Strip. Most of her friends were married with families. She was the last single gal.

"Okay," she said, nodding. "Let's do that."

Jonah grinned. "I'll make all the arrangements, and we'll have some fun."

"Fun. Yes." Did she even remember what fun was?

What could it hurt?

That was a goofy question to ask herself. The last time she briefly pondered something like that she'd ended up being devastated and humiliated. It was simpler not to date. It was easier not to get involved with someone else. Sure, it was lonely, but it was better for her heart in the long run.

"Wow," Jonah said, rocking back on his heels.

"What?"

"You sound like I'm trying to drag you to out into the desert without water."

Oh, little did he know how much she would prefer the desert, and no bodies of water anywhere, but she wasn't going to get into that. Grace cracked a grin and relaxed. "That's a very random statement."

Jonah shrugged. "I was trying to think of the worst thing, but then I realized that's kind of subjective for everyone and I really don't know you well enough to determine what your 'worst thing' would be."

"You want to know my worst thing?"

"Sure."

She'd been teasing, so she was a bit surprised he was so interested. "That's kind of dark, dude."

"Now who sounds like a stereotypical surfer," he teased.

"You're really certain you want to know?"

He nodded. "Lay it on me. I can handle it."

"And you promise you won't use it against me in the future?"

He cocked an eyebrow. "Okay, now I'm absolutely intrigued."

"If I tell you this one thing, then you're going to have to dish out yours."

"Okay, well, how about we share that over a drink?"

She nodded. "We'll do that."

"Come on, let's get back to station and we can go from there."

Grace nodded again and followed her partner across the ambulance bay. She was already feeling so much better. All in all, it had been a good shift. They'd saved a life, and she had helped with that, even if she'd been terrified of running into her ex in the emergency department and the young girl's accident had brought up so many painful memories of her own experience. She'd usually just work this out on her own, but she was appreciative of Jonah for extending her an olive branch of camaraderie.

Friendship with her partner wouldn't be a bad thing. She'd enjoyed working with him so far.

It would be nice to form a closer, professional bond with him.

Wouldn't it?

Why did I suggest this?

Jonah really didn't understand his train of thought when he suggested it, but he also wasn't one to bail. As promised he made all the arrangements. Not many of their coworkers wanted to go out and a couple didn't have the day off tomorrow, but there were a few willing participants, which was good, because he didn't really want to be alone with Grace. Or rather, he wouldn't particularly mind being alone with Grace—quite the opposite, really. And that was the whole crux of the matter.

Grace was exactly the type of woman he was attracted to.

It was going to make being just friends with her tricky. But Jonah had come to Vegas for a fresh start. He'd been married once before, and he didn't want to go through that all again. Keeping people at a distance was easier on him and his pain. He'd already lost too many people he cared about.

His best friend had died in his arms overseas. His parents had been on the older side, never particularly demonstrative, and then they had passed away; he didn't have siblings or really any extended family. His ex-wife hadn't been able to handle his PTSD when he came home, and she had cheated on him. He had learned to rely on himself.

It was better to be alone.

Even if it was lonely.

It was completely out of the ordinary for him to even suggest going out with people from work, but when he'd seen Grace leaning against that wall in the ambulance bay, he'd known a trauma reaction from a mile away, because he'd lived through it. He'd worked through his with amazing therapists. He knew the signs, and it had looked like she needed a shoulder to lean on.

Grace was the perfect partner. She was strong, smart, independent. She could hold her own, and that really impressed him. No one pushed around Grace Landon, and that was just his initial impression after working with her for a few months.

There was a lot about Grace he admired.

So when he'd seen her withdrawn and agitated, it had tugged at his heart because he knew how that felt and how isolating it could be, and he'd had to reach out.

Now, as he rode in a cab to meet his coworkers at a casino bar on the Strip, he was second-guessing his decision to go out and socialize. He was a bit of an introvert—another problem his ex-wife had with him.

In high school, he had been more out there, but his time in service overseas had changed him. After watching so many of his friends get killed, it had been hard to be that "life of the party" type guy his ex, Mona, had expected him to be.

He couldn't do that anymore. He couldn't be that person.

He'd learned to lock away the emotions so that he could control the trauma.

He rolled his shoulders and straightened his white button-down shirt, which was suddenly a little too claustrophobic under his leather jacket. Although he loved living in Vegas, the bright flashing lights and the noise of the Strip was getting to him. Mona would get so annoyed when he'd want to leave an overwhelming social gathering early. She hadn't gotten it.

Not many did.

This night out was his idea, however, and he had to make an effort. Grace had been so keen on it, and he didn't want to let his partner down.

The taxi pulled up in front of Mythtopia Casino, and he made his way inside past all the clouds of cigarette smoke and flashing lights. His pulse raced, and he focused on breathing through the overwhelming overload of sensation. He focused on finding the bar, which was new and located on the upper level of the casino. He'd made reservations so they would have a place to sit and chat.

A quiet place.

When he entered the bar, he was led to a very large corner booth where a few coworkers were sitting. Except Grace, who he'd arranged all this for.

"Hey," Jonah greeted his colleagues. "Where's Grace? Is she running late?"

"No. She's at the bar. She'll be back in a few," John, another paramedic, said, nodding in the direction of the bar before turning back to the others.

Jonah turned and lost his breath for one moment at the sight of Grace seated on a bar stool.

She wore a short silver strapless dress which not only accentuated her long shapely legs but her toned strong arms and shoulders. Her blond hair with that wild pink streak was usually tied back. Now it hung down loose in a bob with subtle waves that brushed the tops of her shoulders.

She was absolutely stunning.

It was the first time he was really seeing her outside of work. Usually, all her curves were hidden by the uniform. Not that she didn't look good that way, but he really appreciated her dressed up like this too. That fact had him slightly rattled. The uniform reminded him she was a partner, someone he worked with, and made it easy to ignore everything else about her.

She's your partner. She's off-limits.

He swallowed the lump in his throat and approached her. Slowly, trying to regain some control over his shock at seeing her looking so different. But it also gave him a chance to savor the sight of her. He wanted to remember this moment, because this was all he could let himself have.

"Hey," he said, hoping that his voice didn't crack.

Grace spun around on the stool and then smiled warmly. "I was wondering if you were going to show up."

"Of course. I was running late." Mostly because he was dragging his feet coming here, but he didn't tell her that. "Why are you sitting off to the side here?"

"John," she grunted, nodding in the direction of the booth. "His stories are the most boring ever."

He smiled. "Yeah, I'd have to agree."

"I'll go back in a few minutes. I was just enjoying my scotch in silence."

She drinks scotch?

For some reason he found that super sexy. She was so different from any other woman he'd met.

"Do you mind if I join you?" he asked.

"Go for it."

Jonah slid onto the barstool next to her. The bartender came over.

"I'll have the same." Jonah motioned to Grace's drink.

"Oh, you like scotch too?"

"It's my favorite. Surprised you do. Most women I've known weren't very fond of it."

She smirked. "Well, I'm not like other women."

He let his gaze travel over her, drinking in the sight of her. "I wouldn't say that."

They sat there in silence and listened to the soft jazz music which was being piped in through the speakers. The bar was decorated in dark colors, dim lighting, leather and wood. It looked like an old smoking room from another time. He actually found in quite calming compared to the loudness of the casino outside. It was why he'd chosen it, so he was glad the pictures online hadn't lied.

"It's like we're in another world here," he said, reaching for the glass the bartender had brought him.

"It's really nice in here," she agreed. "I did wonder about your choice when you picked this casino, but this is a nice little treasure tucked away."

"I did my research. I know tonight is about letting loose, but I also thought it might be nice to actually talk instead of shouting over thumping music."

Their gazes locked, and she smiled at him tenderly as she tucked a lock of her hair behind her ear. "I knew there was a reason I liked you."

"Oh?" he asked, curious.

"I can't stand overly loud obnoxious places either. I mean, it's one thing being in the thick of an emergency and dealing with that. I can usually tune out the sound of the siren blaring, but when I'm off duty I prefer calmness. Quiet."

"Same. After serving in the military..." He trailed off, not wanting to continue with too much information. "When I returned, my tastes had changed."

Her expression softened. "I can only imagine."

"I do like Vegas. I think better than California." Which was true, because there was nothing left for him there. Just painful memories. He closed his eyes for a second as he briefly thought of his past life, before the trauma and divorce. Even once he'd reopened them, the lonely ache in his stomach stayed. It was always present.

"Does anything..." She hesitated for a moment, worrying her bottom lip.

"What?" he asked.

"Does anything trigger you at work?" There was a hint of a flush on her creamy cheeks, almost like she was mortified to be asking him the question, and she shouldn't have been.

Yes, he didn't want to get too close to her. Or anyone, really. But he knew she was suffering today, and he didn't want her to feel the loneliness he'd first felt when he'd returned home from serving in the Marines.

"Things trigger me. I work to control it. Something I've been doing for some time. What about you?" Usually he didn't pry too much, but he had the inkling she wanted to talk about it. That was the point of tonight—giving her a place to talk to him. The others he'd invited so it didn't seem like a date, because it wasn't.

That wasn't what he wanted.

Really?

He ignored that voice in his head. "You can talk to me."

Grace sighed. "I get triggered by drownings. I almost drowned as a child, and... I don't swim or anything like that. Usually I can hold it together, but seeing that little girl in the water... I was about that age when it happened, and I can still remember it with clarity. Days like today, it just hits hard."

"I could tell you were struggling."

She gave him a half smile. "I try to keep it to myself."

"Why?" he asked.

Their gazes locked, and he could see the pain, one he knew too well, reflected back at him.

"People in my life haven't always been too kind or understanding. It's easier to deal with it alone."

Jonah got it, but he found himself wanting to help her, which shocked him. "Who wasn't understanding?"

"My ex. He tried to teach me to swim by dunking my head underwater repeatedly to desensitize me."

Jonah made a face. "What a douche."

Grace laughed. "Well, be careful about that. He's the head trauma doctor at Vegas Central Hospital."

"Did you leave him when he tried that dick move?"

"No, I left him when I found out he was cheating on me with a nurse. Everyone knew but me. Another embarrassing moment of my life that I can't believe I'm telling you." She took a swig of her drink.

Jonah shrugged. "We're partners. And we all have exes we'd rather forget. I was married."

She cocked an eyebrow. "Really?"

"I got married out of high school, and when I got back, things had changed. She wanted someone I wasn't anymore. She cheated on me, it ended and I moved out here...eventually."

He couldn't believe he'd just told her that. It was something he really didn't talk about to anyone. As much as he didn't usually like to open up, with Grace it was easy to do that. It felt as though he was that easygoing guy he'd once been, long before serving. Before Justin had died and Mona had left him. When life had been simple.

Less complicated.

Less painful.

So what was it about Grace? Whatever it was, he'd have to be careful.

"This is turning into a depressing conversation." She smiled at him again. "I'm glad you're letting me talk this all out. When I first met you, you were so closed off."

"I'm careful with who I trust."

Grace nodded. "Me too. Particularly at work."

"Hey, guys! We're going to karaoke at a bar down the street. Come on," John shouted.

Grace winced and then finished her scotch, sliding off the barstool. "We'd better go."

"Had we?" he asked, grumpily.

"This is a coworker-bonding outing, isn't it?" She held out her hand. "Come on. Don't be a curmudgeon."

"A what?"

"A stick in the mud."

Jonah took her hand and slid off the barstool, letting her drag him out of the nice quiet upscale bar.

He could manage one round of karaoke, and then he could go home where it was safe and he could let this social mask slip off and relax.

One round wouldn't hurt him.

CHAPTER TWO

"OH, GOD," GRACE GROANED, not wanting to pry her eyes open to let in more of the sunlight that was already blinding her through her bedroom window. But her phone was ringing incessantly in her dreams, and it was just adding to the pounding that was throbbing against her skull like a bad discotheque. The last time she felt like this she'd been hungover and a lot younger.

What had she been thinking? Why had she drunk so much?

She sat up slowly and realized she was completely naked. At least she was at home and in her bed. She reached for her phone and saw it was her mother calling—and she had been doing so for the last hour, Grace realized as she scrolled through all the missed calls.

Grace ignored the call again, because she was not talking to her mother. Not until she fully woke up. As she scrolled further back, she saw there were about twenty different text messages from her family's group chat.

The chat had been set up by Grace's sister, Melanie—who'd become a bit anal retentive about her upcoming wedding—for sharing details about the event at the end of the month, so that every member of her large family would know what was going on.

Grace tried to regain focus and opened the newest message, which was from her mother.

What do you mean you're MARRIED?!

Grace woke up then. She sat bolt upright in bed, staring at all the texts asking the same question until she found the one that she'd sent. The one that stated she was married. One that had a video attachment.

"Oh, God," she moaned.

There was a shift in the mattress beside her, and she realized in that moment she wasn't alone in the bed. On the pillow next to her were a set of feet and the discernible lump of a human being under her comforter. Her stomach knotted like she was going to throw up. She was pretty sure that wasn't from her hangover.

She gently peeled back the comforter at the foot of the bed to see Jonah sleeping peacefully, his big hand lying flat across his bare, muscular chest with a wedding band on his finger. Grace then noticed there was a matching band on her own hand.

Oh.

My.

God.

She hit Play on the video. It was shaky, so whoever was filming them could've been inebriated too, but there was no mistaking what it showed: her and Jonah, laughing and screaming as they stood at the altar of the Little Wedding Chapel. She only knew it was that particular venue because of the sign behind the officiant.

"John, are you getting this!" she screamed in the video. *"I'm married! Look, Mom. Married. I'm Mrs. Cute Paramedic."*

"And I'm Mr. Cute Paramedic," Jonah slurred.

Grace winced and set the phone down. It began ringing again, but now she *really* couldn't talk to her mother. She buried her face in her hands and then remembered that she was stark naked. She scrambled out of bed and grabbed her robe from where it was hanging up on her closet door, wrapping it around herself quickly. Then she made her way to the other side of the bed and shook Jonah—Mr. Cute Paramedic, apparently—awake.

"Jonah," she said, quietly giving his shoulder a shake.

Jonah answered with a groan, rubbing his face and then he sat up quickly, blinking rapidly. "Where in the hell...?"

"Good morning," she replied, sardonically.

"Grace?" He scrubbed a hand over his face. "What the heck happened last night?"

"After the karaoke? I suppose more drinking and then...a wedding."

Jonah snorted and laughed. "A what?"

She held up her phone and pressed Play. Jonah was smirking, but as he watched their drunken wedding unfold on her phone, his smirk melted away into an expression of horrified realization, and then he noticed his left hand and the new gold band on his ring finger.

Though Grace seriously doubted it was real gold. Especially if it had come from the Little Wedding Chapel at the end of the Strip.

"No," he said in a hushed undertone.

"Yes." She climbed back onto the bed and sat cross-legged across from him. "What are we going to do?"

"Get an annulment?"

"We slept together."

Jonah looked down under the comforter and then realized that he wasn't wearing any clothing. "Well. Damn."

"Damn?" she asked, chuckling slightly at this bizarre situation.

"Not because it was you, but because I can't remember it."

"Neither can I." She rubbed her temples. "My body remembers the alcohol."

"You're dehydrated. You need to drink water." He stood, taking the knotted-up sheet and wrapping it around his waist as he walked out of the bedroom. "I'll get you a remedy for that."

"Thanks," she murmured, watching him in disbelief. It was kind of a surreal situation. Two co-workers married and he was worried about her water intake? It was sweet but made her chuckle at the absurdity of it all.

Jonah came dashing back into her room and shut the door. "There's a person banging on the outside of your condo. I could see their shadow from your living room window."

"What?" She checked her phone to view the door camera she'd set up. It was her mother, and now as she listened, Grace could hear her calling for her faintly from outside to answer the door.

It was mortifying, and she wanted to curl up into a tiny ball and disappear.

Could this day get any worse?

Don't jinx it.

"Do you know who it is?" Jonah asked.

"It's my mother."

His eyes widened. "Your mother?"

She nodded. "Yep."

"Does she live nearby?"

Grace didn't really think that was an important point given the situation, but then again she really wasn't thinking straight either this morning. "She lives in St. George. I guess I texted her last night that we got married. I texted everyone."

Jonah sat back down on the edge of the bed,

looking a bit dumbfounded. There was another sharp rap at the door, and he stood quickly.

"Well," he announced. "I'm not meeting my mother-in-law like this!"

"Your what?"

"Mother-in-law. I suggest we get dressed, Mrs. Cute Paramedic."

Grace chuckled nervously as Jonah moved around the room gathering up his clothing before disappearing into the bathroom. She tried to tame her hair a bit and went to answer the door before her mother broke it down. It was bad enough she'd announced to the whole family she was married, but the fact it was a drunken mistake would disappoint her mother and annoy her already stressed-out little sister. Then would come the inevitable disappointment, which Grace always seemed to provoke when it came to her family.

She let them down. She was a burden.

Her hospital stays after her near drowning when she was a kid had been a financial burden. And her failure to marry Victor, whom her family thought was a good match, deeply disappointed them.

She wished her relationship with Victor had worked out. It had been like a dream being with him, in the beginning.

He was a surgeon, successful, and his best friend was dating her sister. She'd been in love with him.

It had been a fairy-tale romance.

Almost too good to be true.

And that was exactly what it had turned out to be. In the end, it had been more like nightmare than a dream.

Happily-ever-afters just weren't for Grace. She'd learned that lesson well. But her mother wouldn't take that for an answer. Ever since the breakup, she had always nagged Grace about settling down, finding The One.

Now a drunken marriage so close to Melanie's wedding had probably sent her into sheer panic mode.

Worse, Grace knew Melanie would be *so* angry that she was ruining something else. Stealing her sister's thunder, taking away attention and focus from her, just like Grace had done when they were kids. It was a point of contention between the two of them.

She had to make this right somehow.

Grace opened the door. Her mother's eyes were wide and she was holding her phone. Actually, it was more like she was clenching it. "Finally."

"Morning, Mom." Grace stepped aside to let her mom come in out of the heat.

"Morning? It's almost noon."

"It's my day off."

"From what? A honeymoon?" her mother asked.

Grace worried her bottom lip. "Look…"

"No. I'm happy, Grace. After your breakup

with Victor, you were so upset and I never imagined you'd ever find love again. You didn't seem interested."

Grace blinked a couple of times in disbelief. Her mother was...happy? "So, you're okay with this?"

"Why wouldn't I be?"

"So you drove from St. George to Summerlin for that?"

"Well, I'm shocked too. Obviously." Her mother sat down on the couch. "Your sister was beside herself when the news came out. She was at dinner with her fiancé and...his best man."

Grace's stomach sunk. "Melanie and Travis were out with Victor?"

Her mother nodded slowly. "Yep."

Grace groaned. Her mother had never known the full reason why things had ended with Victor. Melanie had already been dating Victor's best friend, the man who'd since become her fiancé, so Grace had kept it all to herself to make peace and never told anyone what happened or how embarrassed she was to be cheated on. At least when she was just running into Victor at the hospital, it had been all business and she could ignore him. Then they'd been put in the wedding party together, and things had stopped being so simple.

And now everyone, including Victor, knew Grace was married. How could she tell her family it was a drunken mistake? Just another humiliating moment to live down.

Maybe it doesn't have to be?

And a wild idea occurred to her. Perhaps Jonah would stay married to her for the month. Just until this big wedding was over, and then they could get a divorce. It would take that long to end it all anyway.

"So?" her mother, asked breaking her erratic chain of thoughts. "Where is my new son-in-law?"

"I'll go get him." Grace dashed from her living room back into the bedroom, causing Jonah to jump slightly. He was doing up his belt. It gave Grace a pause as she got to really appreciate the sight of his tanned, muscle-honed body.

A flash of a hazy memory hit her: her hands running over his chest as he kissed her neck. Heat rushed through her, and all she could do was stare at him.

Jonah paused and cocked an eyebrow. "Grace?"

"Sorry." She pinched the bridge of her nose and shook her head. "My mother is here."

"So you said. Is she angry?"

"No."

"Well, that's good. You're an adult, and mistakes happen."

"About that..."

He crossed his arms. "You say that with hesitation. What's going on?"

Grace wrung her hands together. "We need to pretend to be married. Not a mistake, but for real."

Jonah was shocked, and not for the first time this morning. Waking up married was pretty mind-boggling. He'd vowed to himself, after the divorce from his first wife, that he was never going to let this happen again. Yet here he was.

At least this time it wasn't a rebellion against parents and they weren't straight out of high school. Of course, a drunken elopement with a coworker wasn't exactly any better.

And now here was Grace coming in and asking him to pretend to *stay* married. He had heard her say time and time again at work she wasn't interested in a relationship. So what had changed?

He took a step back and just stared at her, her back against the closed bedroom door, her eyes wide and her hair untamed. She was adorable and disheveled. Bits and pieces of last night were coming back to him, and he was only disappointed that he didn't recall the time they'd spent together with stunning clarity. He had an inkling that was something he'd want to remember.

"What?" he asked, still trying to process it all.

She gulped. "We're married."

"I know."

"And we have to convince my mother that we really are and that it's a good thing and not at all a mistake." She was saying all of this at a mile a minute.

"Why?"

Grace exhaled. "My little sister is getting married."

"Okay, but I don't understand what that has to do with us."

"Her fiancé's best man is my ex, and he knows we're married too. Everyone. Knows." Her cheeks flushed crimson, and she dropped her head into her hands. "This is a disaster."

Jonah moved toward her and put his arm around her, trying to comfort her. She was so soft in his arms, and he remembered this feeling from the night before—wanting to hold her. Part of him wanted to tell her no, because this would muddy the waters at work, and he wasn't here to form any personal attachment. Just work and live out his life...which, when put that way, sounded ridiculously boring. He really did like Grace as a partner—maybe even, one day, a friend—and there was nothing wrong with supporting her. Perhaps he could do this for her, temporarily, even if it went against everything he'd vowed to himself before he moved to Nevada.

So much for keeping your distance.

"So you want to pretend to be married? For how long?"

She grimaced. "A month."

"A month?" he asked, hoping it didn't sound too high pitched as he stepped back.

"I know," she grumbled. "It's a lot."

"It is." He ran his hand through his hair. They'd be together on paper for a month, maybe more anyway, depending on how long it took to fix this situation. There were drive-through wedding booths but no drive-through divorce places he was aware of. He could use one of those right about now.

"What're you thinking?" she asked.

"Okay. As long as it won't affect our work, I can pretend to be your husband to navigate this whole family-wedding thing to help you save face."

Her face relaxed and then lit up, and she threw her arms around him. "Oh, my God. Thank you!"

He held her awkwardly at first, and then he melted into her arms. She felt so good. He had to remember she was not really his.

They were partners.

Partners who were married and about to lie to her family. She stopped clinging to him.

"We can't let this affect our work though." Jonah needed to make that clear. "I want things to stay the same. Professional. I don't want to have to leave Vegas."

"Why would you leave?"

"If it got weird. I don't need that complication in my life."

"Well, I don't want to make it awkward either. So yeah, completely agree—this won't affect our professional relationship."

Even though it seemed unlikely, he kind of believed her. "So I guess I should meet your mother and try to convince her that we're not messing with her?"

"I appreciate you so much." She opened the door.

"Wait! One thing."

She turned around. "What?"

"Your mother's name? I mean, we have to present to her the illusion that we're married and we know each other."

"Good point. Her name is Leslie." Grace opened the door.

Jonah nodded, sucked in a deep, calming breath and walked out of Grace's bedroom to meet her mother.

He still wasn't sure why he'd promised to do this, but he never went back on his word. Especially to a partner.

Except one time…

"I'm not going to make it," Justin grunted.

"Of course you are," Jonah insisted, pulling him tighter, trying to ignore the mortar shell sounds from above.

He was trying so hard to hold on to his wounded

best friend, as if that could save him, but that hope was fleeting.

"I'm not. We're pegged down. Medics are far away," Justin murmured.

"You need to stay awake."

"Don't leave me here, Jonah. Take me home. Promise me. I want to go home."

Jonah swallowed back the tears. "Of course."

He shook that painful reminder away, because it haunted him even after all this time. Jonah hadn't been able to bring Justin home. He'd broken that promise because bombing had started and his best friend's body had been buried under a collapsed tunnel overseas. It ate away at him. It was why he'd left the military; it was another reason why he'd moved to Nevada after his marriage ended, because with his marriage over and Justin dead, there were no ties in California. He had nothing. Nevada was a fresh start.

It was because of Justin, and because of the way Mona had broken her oaths about being faithful to him, that he took promises seriously. And he'd do this for Grace because he liked her and she'd been so kind to him when he'd first arrived. If her family lived in Utah, then he wouldn't see them too much. He'd only have to keep up the act when they were around.

And it was just an act. Grace really wasn't his.

She wouldn't be. Yet he wouldn't do this for just anyone, so why was he doing this for her?

You're hungover and vulnerable. That's why.

"Mom, this is Jonah Crandall. My husband." Grace had plastered a big wide grin on her face and seemed to be talking through her clenched teeth.

Jonah extended his hand out to take the dark-haired, shorter, older version of Grace by the hand. "Pleasure to meet you, Mrs. Landon."

"You can call me Leslie. We're family," Leslie gushed. "It's nice to meet you, although we were all shocked by the surprise. We couldn't quite believe it."

"As were we," Jonah replied, slipping his arm around Grace's shoulders and pulling her rigid body closer.

"Well, why don't we go out and have a nice lunch somewhere?" Leslie offered.

"Don't you have to shop for dinner tonight?" Grace asked.

Leslie waved her hand dismissively. "I can shop and get home in time."

"Well, actually Jonah has to go back to his place," Grace explained quickly.

Leslie looked confused. "His place? Doesn't he live here?"

Jonah glanced down at Grace, who seemed to be doing a good job of digging a hole with her perceptive mother. "I will be. Soon. Moving in tomorrow. Everything about us is a bit…muddled. Besides that. We've been planning my moving in for a couple of months."

His insides clenched at the lie. Maybe Grace wasn't the only one digging a big old hole for themselves. He seemed to be doing a good job too.

Leslie smiled. "Well, that makes sense. Maybe I will get the shopping done early, in that case. There's a big family dinner tonight in St. George. We have a lot to discuss about Melanie's wedding, and Grace, you are a bridesmaid—you should be there. Now you can bring Jonah, because I'm sure everyone wants to meet this mystery man you raced to the altar with."

"We'll be there," Jonah answered while Grace gave him a slightly crazed look. And he didn't blame her. He was surprised at himself for suggesting it as well, because it was the last thing he wanted to do.

"Good." Leslie headed toward the door. "I'll finish my errands and head back to Utah. I'll see you both tonight at six."

Grace let her mother out of her condo and then spun around to face him. "Why did you agree to that?"

"The family dinner? I assumed you were going."

"No." Grace sat down on the couch. "My family can be a little over the top."

"Are they super religious or something?"

"Several of them are LDS—Mormon. But we're

married, so they won't blink an eye about living together," Grace replied. "I'm not religious."

"Well, you wanted to pretend we're married, so let's go and convince them of that fact."

Grace chewed on the bottom of her lip and didn't look convinced at first. Her whole body was tense, like she was on edge. "I don't know."

"Come on—you know if you want them to believe you, you'll have to go to dinner."

Her shoulders dropped, and she let out a sigh. "You're right. You know my mom will be popping in after this...to check on us."

"I'll move in." And he couldn't believe he said that out loud, that it was his idea.

What is happening to me?

Grace's eyes widened. "What about your place?"

"I've been living at vacation and short-term rentals since I got here."

"For six months?"

Jonah shrugged. "I was waiting to find the perfect place and save money. I can sleep on your couch."

Grace wrung her hands together for a moment, glancing at her couch. "If you're okay with this, then of course. I did put you on the spot."

"You're not totally to blame for this marriage. We both had too much to drink when we said our *I do*s."

Grace chuckled softly. "I suppose."

"I'll go pack up my stuff, get cleaned up, and I'll be back in time for us to head to St. George and face your family."

"You're being super supportive. I can't thank you enough."

"Of course. It's what good partners do. They back each other up."

Something Justin and he had always said when they went through basic training together. It was something he continued to live by.

"That's a good practice. I like that," she agreed.

"Try not to worry." Which he knew was easier said than done. He opened the door and stepped outside to call a cab as the reality of what was happening sunk in.

His marriage to Grace wasn't a forever situation, but right now they were legally tied together while they got their paperwork done, so why not have some fun and show her ex she'd moved on? He'd worked with Grace long enough to know she was professional and wouldn't let this affect their partnership. He'd believed her when she reassured him of that.

He could keep this whole marriage platonic, even if it had been kind of nice to wake up next to her this morning. Scary, but nice all the same. Jonah touched his lips as he remembered the softness of her kisses, her sweet taste and thought of how he wouldn't mind experiencing it all again without the haziness of alcohol. Only he couldn't give in. He had to remind himself of the fact that he'd tried marriage once before with someone he thought he knew, and it had ended so badly.

He was never going to put his heart on the line again.

No matter how much Grace tempted him.

CHAPTER THREE

GRACE CHECKED HER watch nervously, which was just a fidgety nervous reaction. She was freaking out about going to this dinner and facing her family. The last thing she wanted to do was be late, but she was being silly. They had plenty of time to make the almost two-hour trip to St. George. Jonah had texted her that he would be back to her place by three thirty so they could get on the road and head to her family's home.

Her phone had been pinging all morning with messages from various family members, some who were going to be at dinner tonight and some who weren't, all questioning her and wondering about Jonah.

Her mother had hopped on the group chat and let all those curious family members know that she had met Jonah, thought he was really nice and good looking and that he was coming to dinner that night.

Melanie hadn't said much. Well, except for insinuating that Grace had rushed to beat her to the altar, hinting that her big sister was once again deliberately stealing the spotlight. Their mother had jumped in and shut it down, but as with all their childhood fights since the near drowning, Melanie would just see that as their parents protecting Grace once again. It made Grace feel so guilty. She really didn't mean to infringe on Melanie's big day.

She'd never even planned on getting married. After what happened with Victor, Grace had a hard time believing in happily-ever-afters. He had said he loved her but cheated on her. How was that love? She wouldn't let herself ever go through that kind of hurt again.

At least Victor wouldn't be at the family dinner tonight, but she'd see him soon enough as the wedding crept closer.

Please be short-staffed and call Jonah and me in to work.

It was the mantra that she was repeating over and over in her head, but it wasn't working.

Usually, she loved her days off, especially after a long rotation on shift, but right now she wouldn't mind being called into the station and avoiding the awkwardness that awaited her in St. George.

A cab rolled up, and Jonah got out. He pulled out a large suitcase and a duffel bag before waving the cab driver off. She was shocked that Jonah had his whole life in two bags. Apparently, he was very minimalistic, whereas she was bit of a hoarder when it came to nice clothes, workout clothes—really any kind of clothes—and shoes. Plus bags... It was a good thing he hadn't looked into her large walk-in closet.

Why are you thinking about that now? Focus.

"You don't have a car?" she asked as she flung open the door to greet him as he climbed the steps to her condo.

"I have a motorcycle, but since you don't have a garage at your complex I decided to put it into a little storage unit I have. To keep it safe."

The idea of Jonah on a motorcycle sent of ripple of thrill down her spine. She could imagine him sitting astride it, dressed in leather and traveling across the desert.

With me on the back?

The suggestion from her brain surprised her. She'd never even ruminated on the idea of going on a motorcycle before. Yet picturing Jonah and wrapping her arms around him kind of titillated her.

"I've never seen you ride to work on your bike," she mused, trying to clear the image of him and her riding off into the Nevada sunset together.

"No, I don't usually ride it to the station. I've always had rentals that were close by. I can still walk from here," he said, glancing around. "Summerlin isn't far."

"It's far enough. I'll drive you in. We work the same shifts anyway."

He nodded curtly. "Deal."

"So that's all you have? Just a couple of bags?"

"Well, a few boxes in storage, but yeah, I travel light. I learned that in the military. When I got divorced my ex kept everything, and I had no problem with that. I wanted to leave California."

"Do your parents know about our little mishap?" she asked, taking the suitcase from him to walk it into her condo.

"No." He slung his duffel bag over his shoulder.

"Should you tell them?" she queried, alarmed by his nonchalant answer.

"Nope."

"Are you sure you didn't drunkenly text them too?"

"No, because…" He hesitated and sighed. "My parents are long gone. They were older when I was born. And no, I don't have siblings. I was their only child."

"I didn't mean to pry. You seem bugged by telling me that."

"No. I just… I like to keep things to myself. I'm kind of private."

"I've noticed," she mused.

"It's fine," he said tightly. Somehow she didn't think it was, and she felt guilty for questioning him.

"I'm sorry." She moved to the side so he could drop his bag in her living room.

"It's okay. I guess you should know in case it all comes up. Dad died while I was overseas and I lived with my mom for a bit after my marriage ended, but she died within a year of my returning. She was eighty. I was a surprise baby." She spotted a twinkle in his eyes. "I miss them."

"No other family?" she asked, thinking about her own large family and how involved they were in her life.

"Nope. They were only children too. I never knew my grandparents. There were no cousins. It was the three of us for a long time."

She couldn't even begin to contemplate the idea of such a small family.

Of being alone.

Aren't you alone now, Grace?

Suddenly she felt really guilty for wanting to get out of this dinner with her family. Jonah's story made her appreciate them. They were numerous and got in her business, but she was glad she had them. "Well, are you ready for this? I mean, you're not used to a large, in-your-face family. Some of them, the Mormon ones, are quiet, but for the most part they really like to be in each other's business."

Jonah laughed, but there was a nervous edge to it. "I think so. It'll be fine."

"You say that with such confidence."

"They'll ask the conventional questions about how we met... Well, that's easy—we met at work. I think we can handle mostly everything. We've both seen the unfortunate video, and they've seen it too. We'll stick with what I told your mother—we've been thinking about it for some time, and it just happened."

"You're so calm about this," Grace teased.

"Believe me, I'm not that calm. I prefer solitude."

"I do too."

"Is that why you moved away from Utah?"

"Bingo."

He smiled slightly and looked away. "We'll get through this."

"I'm a nervous wreck."

He cocked his head to one side. "I've never seen this side of you. When you're at work or in the station house you're, like, no-nonsense."

She smiled. "Lives are on the line at work. I take it seriously. Whereas with my family, sometimes I get close to losing my cool and then I might actually have to call in a paramedic to help."

Jonah laughed quietly to himself. "I'll forget you said that."

"Just you wait. Do you need anything before we leave?" she asked.

"Nope. I'm ready." He opened her door, and she locked it behind them. They headed back down to the parking lot and to her car.

"Is that pool for everyone?" he asked offhandedly.

Grace's body stiffened. "Yep. You can use it whenever you want. I have a key card."

"Great."

What she didn't tell him was she had never used the condo's community pool. Not once since she moved in. She'd tried to find a place without a pool, but it was difficult to find in this area.

Mostly, she just ignored its existence when she walked by it.

She relaxed once it was behind them and they got to her car.

Jonah climbed in and buckled up. Grace thought again about how much she would have loved to show up on the back of his motorcycle, clad in leather, to a family dinner. It would definitely turn some heads. But she really didn't mind driving. As the senior partner, she was often the one who sat in the driver's seat of the rig at work, and it felt right to have Jonah seated next to her. Except now there was an awkward tension that settled between them. The silence had never bothered her before. Now it felt different, probably because of the lie and the sex.

Memories of that were coming back to her,

and it was hard not to think on it when it had felt so good.

"Is that a pie?" he asked, peering in through the rearview mirror.

"It is."

"I didn't know you baked."

"I don't, but there's a bakery down the street that does."

Jonah leered. "That's disappointing."

"That's a bit chauvinistic…expecting a woman to bake!" she goaded good-naturedly.

He laughed, his eyes glinting. "That's not what I mean. I was excited to learn a hidden talent about you, wife."

"It's not 'wife.' It's Mrs. Cute Paramedic, I believe."

"Oh, Lord," he groaned. "I'm sorry about that."

"It wasn't you. I think it was me."

"It's a terrible name."

She rolled her eyes but couldn't help smirking. That awkward tension she'd been feeling a moment ago melted away with some easy banter. They drove away from Summerlin and headed out onto the Bruce Woodbury Beltway, which connected to the interstate leading them through Arizona and then into Utah.

Grace was dreading what lay in store for them there.

Her family.

And a whole lot of questions.

At least it was a nice day for a drive, and riding with Jonah was a breeze. They were conversing freely, a bit more freely now, even than when they were at work. It never really bothered Grace that Jonah kept to himself a lot of the time at work; he was a good partner. But she also kind of liked this chattier side of him. Hopefully he wouldn't be too annoyed with her for forcing the conversation by asking way too many questions.

It surprised her how nice it felt having someone to talk to. She hadn't realized how solitary her life had become. There was no time for friends when she worked so much. Work was her life.

"You look distressed," Jonah remarked.

"Do I?" she asked, gripping the steering wheel a bit tighter.

"Your knuckles are going white."

Grace relaxed a bit. "Just mentally bracing for what's to come."

"Don't fret about it. Believe it or not, I'm quite charming."

She glanced over him and laughed. "What?"

"I can be social when I want to. I did arrange that work get-together."

"True. I suppose you're responsible for this whole mess."

Jonah frowned. "What do you mean?"

"It was your idea to get married."

"Pardon?" he asked.

"I distinctly remember you asking me to marry you after our duet at karaoke."

"I think you asked me. After you grabbed my butt," Jonah countered.

Grace's mouth dropped open. "I would never do such a thing."

"You did. Several times."

Heat flushed into her cheeks, and little bits of last night came back to her. She had been a bit handsy with him. "I will concede I was the one who initiated the kiss."

That she definitely remembered.

And her stomach fluttered in excited remembrance of how she had pulled his hard body against her. How good it had been to melt right into that kiss. She couldn't remember ever feeling that way with Victor. It had been hot, but with Jonah it had been something she'd never experienced before. She wanted more.

You're partners, remember?

And she had to keep that thought in her head. Jonah agreed to this whole arrangement on the condition that it didn't affect their working relationship, and she'd promised him it wouldn't. So she couldn't let herself even entertain the idea of touching him or kissing him.

She had to put that all out of her mind.

The drive to St. George was good. Jonah didn't mind long rides. The best thing in the world to help him relax was to get onto his motorcycle and ride across the desert. It was a way to connect himself to the elements, so it wasn't exactly the same in a car, but it was still nice to enjoy the scenery and engage in pleasant conversation with Grace.

And that shocked him. The last time he'd been this at ease was when he'd originally been dating his ex. Before his time in the service had changed him. Before Mona had changed.

It was hard not to talk to Grace.

And talking about nothing kept his thoughts off the fact that she was wearing a very cute and flattering sun dress. It went past her knees, but he knew very well all the curves that were hidden underneath the flowery, breezy fabric and how they had felt under his hand as he'd traced the lines of her body when they were naked together in her bed.

Get a grip.

It was hitting him how fast he'd agreed to this fake marriage. Why? Why hadn't he just walked away? It would have made it so much easier to keep his desire for Grace at bay.

Maybe because he was lonely.

Really, he had no one left. His parents were gone, his first marriage had been over for years, Justin was dead.

In California he'd spent years healing and closing himself off. Grace was like a breath of fresh air. It was scary, this lying and pretending, but maybe it would be fun to be included in some family normality.

Or maybe a bit of abnormality if what Grace was saying about her family was true.

"We're almost there," Grace said, breaking in on his reflections. There was a nervous edge to her voice, and she was gripping the steering wheel again.

"It'll be okay," he reassured, but truth be told he was starting to feel a bit nervous too. Never mind the lie they were telling, socializing with crowds of people bothered him enough. Did he even really know how to be that same person he used to be? The last thing he wanted to do was snap or have a moment where he lost control in front of complete strangers.

It won't be like that.

He only hoped his inner voice was right.

Leslie Landon had been really nice and pleasant, even in spite of the fact he'd drunkenly married her daughter, but he couldn't help but think about the rest of the family. What would they think of him?

Mona's family had never been keen on him. Even when he and Mona had been dating in high school. Probably because they'd eloped right after they graduated and Jonah had enlisted the day after their wedding. Now he knew that leaving her alone so soon hadn't been the best move as a supportive husband. He'd thought their love would be enough to sustain them, but it hadn't been.

Marriage was a two-way street, a partnership. It took work. He'd realized that too late. When he'd gotten back from deployment, he'd tried to heal the rift that had grown between them. Instead of working on it with him, Mona had cheated, then demanded the divorce.

The day of the divorce he'd lost what little family he had.

Thankfully, his mother had been around. She hadn't been crazy about Mona either, but she was the support he'd needed then. He missed her.

Mom would've liked Grace.

Warmth spread from the center of his chest as he pictured his mom meeting Grace. Just thinking about it made him happy. His mom definitely would've liked her. Even in the few months that he'd known Grace, he could see similar personality traits in her, and that softened him.

You have to be careful, his inner voice warned.

Thinking like that made him vulnerable.

"Right. It'll be okay," Grace responded nervously. "However, I do have a strong sensation like there's a flock of birds taking up resident in the pit of my stomach."

"Tell me about your family. I know your mom, Leslie, but tell me about the others. Who else will I be meeting?" Maybe if he focused on names and details, he wouldn't worry so much.

Grace took a deep breath. "Well, there's my dad, Rick. He might be a little hard on you. He's protective of his daughters. Then again, he calls me tough cookie. I was a bit of a tomboy."

Jonah smiled. "I can believe that. Who else?"

"The bride-to-be is my younger sister, Melanie. She's two years younger than me, and honestly, we're polar opposites. She's a bit of a princess, and I'm pretty sure she's angry with me for getting married. Her fiancé is Travis."

"And his best man is your ex?"

"Yes," Grace said, stiffly. "Victor."

"The surgeon, right?"

"Yes. At least he won't be there tonight," she groused.

"Anyone else?"

"My little brother, Aidan. He's sixteen. He was a surprise to my parents."

"Oh, so we have that in common." They shared a smile, and he tore his gaze away. "So, Leslie, Rick, Aidan, Melanie and Travis?"

"And our elderly, neurotic dog, Pepper. She's a golden doodle."

"A what?" he asked.

"Golden retriever and standard poodle. A golden doodle."

"Okay. Sounds good."

"There might be extended family there, but I don't know." Grace gripped the wheel again as she flicked her blinker on and turned off the interstate. "Welcome to St. George."

Southern Utah was different from all the pictures he'd seen of Utah, which usually involved the Salt Lake area farther north. St. George resembled Nevada and Arizona but with beautiful red rock vistas. There were gorgeous palm trees, and it looked to be a happening city. Not as big as Vegas, but a nice place to live.

Grace didn't say much as she navigated the streets. They made their way to an affluent middle-class neighborhood, and she parked in front of a modern brick bungalow home in the subdivision of Bloomington, on a corner lot that overlooked the red rock hills. It had a beautifully manicured desert garden and stonework out front and a triple garage. The wide boulevards were lined with lush green trees.

It was serene. Like something out of a magazine. Maybe it was almost too picture perfect.

There was a young man outside on the driveway shooting hoops, and Jonah had a suspicion this was Grace's younger brother, Aidan.

Grace took a deep breath. "Here we go."

"I'll grab the pie." Maybe if he was holding on to that, he wouldn't want to bolt.

She nodded, and they climbed out of her car.

"Grace!" Aidan called, his basketball under one arm as he came running over to give her a side hug.

"Hey, Aidan. How's the mood inside?" Grace asked.

Aidan shrugged. "As expected. Melanie is freaked out!"

Grace inhaled another deep breath. "Jonah, this is my little brother, Aidan. Aidan, this is Jonah, my…"

"Your husband," Aidan grinned, his eyes twinkling. "Oh, I know!"

Grace groaned.

"It's nice to meet you," Jonah said.

"It's nice to meet you too. Prepare to be grilled. Grandma and Grandpa are in there, as well as Auntie Gert. Plus some of the wedding party."

Grace's expression dropped. "Some of the… what?"

Aidan was indifferent to his sister's change in tone, but Jonah was aware.

"You know, Melanie's maid of honor and the best man with his wife. Mom wants to talk about the wedding. I'm escaping all that boring talk until dinner." Aidan jogged back to his basketball hoop.

Grace nodded, and Jonah could sense the anxiety melting off her. Without even thinking about it, he reached down and took her hand, squeezing it.

"It'll be okay," he reassured gently.

"Will it?" she asked, her voice breaking slightly.

"If not, I can always pie him." He was surprised

at the suggestion—and the way he found himself waggling his eyebrows—but it made Grace laugh, and that was all that mattered. This wasn't going to be easy for either of them, but it would be best to get it all over and done with. "Come on. Let's get this over, then."

She nodded, and they walked up the driveway to her front door. She was still trembling, but she didn't let go of her death grip on him. Jonah remembered clearly having to deal with Mona and the man she cheated on him with. Mona hadn't ended up marrying the other man, but Jonah knew exactly how Grace was feeling. It had been humiliating.

And he was dead serious about shoving a pie into her ex's face if he got out of hand.

He had a wife to protect, even if she was fake.

For the next month, she was his—something he'd never thought he'd say to himself ever again.

CHAPTER FOUR

KNOWING VICTOR WAS HERE, all Grace wanted to do was run. When she opened up the front door of her parents' home and stepped in, it felt like she was walking the plank to her own demise.

Instantly, she felt bad for Jonah—really bad, because she was putting him in a precarious situation. Well, maybe *precarious* was putting it too strongly, but if the situations had been reversed, she'd be nervous as heck. Jonah had plastered on a million-dollar reality-television kind of smile—fake and really, really big. It was almost comical. She was kind of glad that he was too pretty for his own good, something she always thought when she looked at him and his classic California good looks. Right now, it worked to her advantage; as far as she was concerned, Jonah was definitely more attractive than Victor. And that gave her a small amount of petty, devious pleasure.

"Mom?" she called out, hoping that her voice didn't shake. "We're here."

Her mother came rushing out of the back,

where the sunroom was. It was where they entertained guests. She looked flustered, but then again she'd always been something of a whirlwind.

"You both made it," her mother said, quickly letting out a big breath of air.

"Did you have doubts?" Grace asked.

"I did."

"I said I would be here," Grace replied.

"I wasn't sure," her mother said in a hushed undertone. "Melanie is having a slight meltdown."

Grace knew exactly how that felt in a way, because she was on the verge of having one herself. "Why?" she asked.

Her mother made a face, as if to say *You should know*, and Grace's stomach knotted up into a tight little ball. Her sister was upset by her drunken elopement with Jonah. Coming here tonight had been a bad idea.

"I brought pie. Or rather, we brought pie," Jonah piped up, breaking the tension which had descended.

"How thoughtful of you." Her mother took the pie from Jonah. "I'll take care of this, and Grace can introduce you to the rest of the family."

"Family. Right," Grace muttered as she took Jonah's leather jacket to hang up in the closet by the front door. Her mother scurried off to the kitchen.

"How are you so calm with this?" Grace hissed under her breath.

"I'm not," Jonah whispered back. "Fake it till you make it."

"I'll run if you want to," Grace suggested.

"Don't act so eager," Jonah teased as she put his jacket on a hanger. "We can do this."

"What?"

"You act like you're going to your own funeral."

"Aren't we?"

"Maybe."

She chuckled and shut the door, leaning against it. "I feel like I might be."

"It went fine with your brother, and I'm sure this will be okay too." There was an edge to his voice like he was trying to give himself a pep talk.

"Aidan's a sixteen-year-old boy. My sister is a bride, and she might even be that more mythical creature."

Jonah cocked an eyebrow. "And what's that?"

"Bridezilla," Grace whispered, though she couldn't help but grin as she said it.

Jonah snickered and playfully rolled his eyes. "Great," he snorted. "I can handle that."

"You say that with sincerity."

"Come on—we'd better go in there holding hands. Show our solidarity against all those monsters," he joshed.

Grace glanced down at his outstretched palm. She was not a touchy-feely type of person, but seeing him offering unanimity made her calm, and she gladly took his warm, strong hand in her own. It was support, an anchor she hadn't known she needed until that moment. She was sure she was shaking, but having him here was grounding. Especially when she knew she was perpetuating a lie of her own doing. Even if he was just as nervous as her, it felt like they were together as a team. In this moment Jonah was her rock to stand on, and she really appreciated him.

As she approached the sunroom, she could hear the voices of her family: the high-pitched excited sound of her sister, followed by Travis, her future brother-in-law, trying to calm her. Yeah, it was clear to Grace that her nuptials weren't being very well received.

And she felt bad about that.

It was never her intention to encroach on her sister's wedding, let alone marry her partner after a drunken night of karaoke. Her situation was like something out of a sitcom from the eighties or nineties.

Surreal. That was the word.

"Hi, everyone." Grace knew her voice broke as she said those words. Jonah gave her hand a reassuring squeeze, and she returned it.

Everyone in that room turned their heads slowly and stared at her. Melanie, who had been perched on the arm of her fiancé's chair, stood up and crossed her arms.

"Hi yourself," she stated through pursed lips.
Yep. Definitely mad.

Jonah squeezed her hand again in reassurance. As if he could sense it too.

"This is my…my husband, Jonah." It was hard to get those words out.

"Hi," Jonah greeted brightly. It was completely unlike the real him that Grace knew, but then again when he was on the job he could be very personable with patients and their families.

She held her breath, waiting for someone to say something.

Anything.

No one said a word. She could have heard a pin drop in that room.

"Jonah, is it?" Victor asked, breaking the silence finally. "Aren't you a paramedic?"

It was an innocent-enough question, but it made Grace clench her free hand into a fist, because she knew Victor's view on paramedics. It was nothing short of egotistical for him to think that way. Paramedics might not have gone to school as long as trauma doctors like him, but what they did was vital. It was something she and Victor had argued about often enough.

She knew Victor's wife agreed with him on the superiority of doctors. He'd always needed constant praise. Honestly, years later, Grace realized she should've seen that as the red flag it really was.

"I am. Grace and I are partners. That's how we met. So glad I work with her. She's the best partner." Jonah brought Grace's hand up to his mouth and kissed it. The moment his lips touched her skin, need raced through her, settling deep in her belly as some fragments of memories from the drunken wedding night ran through her brain.

His lips on more than her hand.

The pleasure she'd experienced with him.

She knew her cheeks were red because she could feel the heat, the desire burning through her blood. In that moment, it was just the two of them in that room and she forgot about everyone else.

Victor didn't say anything else. No one did. They all stood there, staring.

"I'm glad I work with you too," Grace said softly, meeting his gaze.

Victor snorted. Just slightly, but Grace heard it.

Apparently, Jonah did too. His eyes narrowed in on Victor. "She's one of the best paramedics in Vegas. I'm proud to work with her and I'm proud to be married to her."

He was standing up for her. Despite the fact that he didn't even know her family. She appreciated it. No one really did that for her—not that she would have let them—and the fact Jonah had was making her heart beat just a bit faster. She had been dreading all these get-togethers, and there was a small fraction of her that was uneasy about forcing Jonah to go ahead with this charade, but right now, she wasn't regretting anything. In this moment she felt strong with him by her side.

"Well, I guess congratulations are in order," Travis said, standing up and extending his hand to shake Jonah's.

"Thanks, Travis." Grace gave her future brother-in-law a quick hug.

Melanie was frowning, but she hugged Grace. "I'm happy for you."

"I'm happy for you too," Grace responded.

"I'm glad you came tonight. I was worried you wouldn't," Melanie admitted, her eyes darting quickly over to Victor.

"I'm here. You have to be excited about wedding planning. Right?"

Melanie nodded. "I am."

Grace pulled her sister aside. "I didn't mean to steal your thunder."

She wanted to make things right for Melanie. She really hadn't done this on purpose.

Melanie relaxed. "I know. And I know it's hard for you with Victor. I was…shocked when I saw that video sent to the wedding chat."

"So was I," Grace said, chuckling. "I won't let this ruin your day. Okay?"

Melanie nodded.

There was a loud bang from the hall that made them all jump. The front door, slamming.

"Aidan?" her mom called out. "Do you have to slam every door in the house?"

"Help!" Aidan shouted as he came busting in the room. "Mr. Petersen next door collapsed walking his dog."

Grace didn't even hesitate. She ran after her brother with Jonah close behind her and Victor following even closer. She told her mother to call emergency services. When she got outside there was a crowd gathered at the end of the driveway.

"Did someone call the paramedics?" Jonah shouted over his shoulder as they dropped down next to the unconscious man lying on the ground. She wasn't even sure if she heard anyone reply, because calling for backup wasn't her focus. Someone in her family would definitely take care of it. Instead, all her attention went to the patient. She'd learned in situations like this how to block out everyone else and focus completely on her work.

Even when in situations that got to her, like drownings, it was never until her adrenaline had dipped that she crashed and was laid flat on her ass.

"I told my mother to call," Grace answered.

"His pupils are reacting. That's good. How is his airway?" Victor asked as he flashed a small penlight he carried everywhere into Mr. Petersen's eyes. He was checking the man's pupils, and she was glad he carried that little light around, because the sun was setting and it was very dark at the end of the driveway.

"Clear," Jonah said, checking the man's throat. They got him onto his back.

"His pulse is thready," Grace remarked. "Shine that light on his hands, Victor."

Victor did, and she immediately assessed that there was a bluish tinge to the nail beds, which definitely meant there was a lack of oxygen. It could've been a coronary, it could've been a stroke, but she wasn't a doctor and couldn't speculate.

Mr. Petersen was breathing, and that was the main thing.

"Mr. Petersen?" Jonah called out loudly. "Can you hear us?"

There was no response, but Grace could hear the distant wail of the St. George paramedics on their way. This was their jurisdiction, their hospitals, and she didn't have the equipment. At least he would get help.

The paramedics arrived, and they helped get Mr. Petersen loaded up into the ambulance. Jonah stood back with her as Victor, the physician, spoke with the local emergency medical workers. Jonah was frowning as he watched the whole thing.

"What's wrong?" she asked.

"I hate stepping away from a job," he murmured, and then a half smile tugged on his lips. "I like to see a job through and make sure the person is okay. I guess it stems back from my military training."

"Then how would that explain me?"

Jonah cocked an eyebrow. "What?"

"I feel the same, and I wasn't in the military."

He smiled down at her tenderly. "I knew there was a reason I liked you."

"Well, that's something at least."

The doors of the ambulance slammed shut, and the crowd was dispersing. The siren let out a wail and then drove away.

"Well, that was a bit unexpected," Grace's mother said. "Hopefully Mr. Petersen will be okay. Good thing you were on the scene, Victor."

Grace tried not to roll her eyes, but then her mother turned to them.

"And both of you…as well," her mother explained.

"I'm glad we were here too, Mrs. Landon," Jonah responded. "All of us."

Her mother smiled at Jonah. "Well, dinner is ready, and there's nothing more we can do here."

Jonah reached down and took Grace's hand again, squeezing it reassuringly, and Grace returned the gesture. This whole thing might've been a ruse, but with Jonah, the right partner, she could overcome this.

Jonah had sensed that awkward tension the moment they walked into that sunroom. It had grated on him. It was the absolute worst, and he tried so hard to take it just so everyone would buy into their act. Especially seeing how Grace's ex was there. And he'd recognized Victor right away. He was a good trauma doctor but kind of a snobby jerk. There was another word that Jonah could use, but he wouldn't let himself actually think it because even thinking it would be pushing the line just a bit.

He really didn't see what Grace had seen in Victor, but then again he'd asked himself the same questions time and time again about Mona. He had been a different person then, and he was pretty sure the same would be true of Grace.

He didn't know that version of her. He barely knew the current version of Grace beyond work, because he hadn't intended to get to know *anyone*. So much for that plan.

Honestly, he was still trying to wrap his brain around the fact that he'd agreed to this whole marriage-of-convenience thing, something that he assumed was only done in romance novels. But here he was, living the dream.

And that was how he had to keep his focus— thinking of it as a fun dream, not a nightmare. If he didn't try to put a positive spin on it all, he wouldn't be able to keep up their charade of being husband and wife. In fact, he'd probably run for the hills, because marrying for real and trying to make a life with someone else relying on him was not in his cards.

There was no way he was ever going to put any

piece of himself out on the line for someone and get hurt again.

Reminding himself that this was all a fake while they waited for the divorce had helped him play along, because he truly did like Grace and he wanted to be friends with her. He wanted to be able rely on her as a partner.

Surprisingly, it had been easy to turn on that Californian charm when he'd walked into her family house and met everyone. And the fact that a neighbor had had a medical emergency hadn't even fazed him.

That he could deal with, but now sitting around a large dining room table with a bunch of people he didn't know, people who had multiple questions for him, was a bit nerve wracking. That urge to bolt came over him again. It was crowded, claustrophobic, and he was stuck right in the middle of a bunch of strangers.

Case in point: meeting Aunt Gert, who wore her black mascara *really* thick. He was trying hard not to stare at the clumps collecting in the corners of her eyes as she ogled him. Grace had noticed and was endeavoring not laugh.

Traitor.

He tried to focus in on the wedding chatter, but it was difficult because he was not interested in it.

"We're getting married at the country club," Melanie piped up. "I have a wedding coordinator, and it's going to be outdoor and elegant."

Grace's nose wrinkled at the mention of the country club, and Jonah wondered why.

"Do you golf a lot, Travis?" he asked, trying to make conversation because he hated the awkwardness of being seated at this table. Grace's father, Rick, still wouldn't even look him in the eye. He was the one person who Jonah really hadn't met because when they'd briefly been introduced, Rick just nodded stiffly at him. Jonah remembered what Grace had told him—that her father could be overprotective.

If Jonah had daughters he might be too.

He shook that thought away. He was never going to have a family—ever. Why dwell on it?

"I do," Travis said. "Right, Rick?"

"We do," Rick answered. "In fact, we're coming down to Vegas in a week to do a bachelor thing for Travis. We're going golfing and having a steak dinner. Jonah, you should join us."

Jonah was shocked by the invite. And he couldn't really tell if it was genuine or not. It sounded almost as if it was perfunctory.

Grace's eyes flew open. "Dad, you don't..."

"No, it's no trouble. He's your husband," Rick stated firmly. "I need to get to know him."

Jonah's stomach knotted.

"I would love to. Just let me know where and when." He actually despised golfing, had never played it and found it boring to watch, but it would seem kind of rude and suspicious not to accept the invitation, since he'd been the one to bring up the sport. And he'd brought it up because he associated golf with country clubs.

"Great," Rick said. "We'd love to have you since you're a member of the family now."

But Jonah wasn't sure how much *love* was really in that statement. It was a nice sentiment, but it seemed kind of forced.

"Right." He swallowed the hard lump in his throat. Part of the family? No, he really wasn't, but there was an appeal to being included in a family again.

It had been so long.

Even though his parents had been a bit distant with him because they'd been older, he'd never been lacking in love while they'd lived. But they'd been gone for a few years now. It had been some time since he'd had a chance to bask in a family environment. He kind of liked it.

He missed it.

Don't let yourself think like that.

Since he planned to live alone the rest of his life, he couldn't let himself get attached to anything. Last time he'd done that had been with Mona's family. They might not have really warmed up to him or liked him, but they'd been there and supportive. Until the marriage had ended—then they had completely shut him out.

He lost his best friend, his wife and his parents

all in a short amount of time. Those were dark years, and he was never going back to that.

He had to keep his distance from Grace and her folks so when this pretense was over and they went back to being nothing more than partners, it wouldn't hurt so much.

The rest of the dinner passed in a blur, and everyone ate the pie that Grace had brought. Once the meal was over, he found himself sitting outside alone and staring up at the clear night sky. You couldn't see many stars, because St. George was a city just like Vegas, but it was a bit darker here and they were higher in elevation, so there were a couple popping out.

The quiet and the stars helped him refocus and not let those past hurts take over. Even if he was concerned about the upheaval of his emotions, he'd made a promise to Grace and he wouldn't back out now, especially after meeting her family.

"There you are," Grace said, quietly slipping through the sliding glass door.

"Yeah, I wanted a few moments of peace before we hit the road."

She nodded. "Contemplating your choice about golfing with my dad, maybe?"

Jonah slightly lifted his shoulders. "Maybe."

"Do you even know how to golf?"

"No. Do you?"

"I do."

He was taken aback. "You do?"

"Why are you so shocked by that? A lot of women play golf. I actually enjoy it."

"You like golf?" He made a face and shook his head. "Seems kind of boring."

"It's not, and it's clear I'm going to have to give you some golf lessons before you get out on the green with my dad, Travis and Victor."

He groaned. "Victor too?"

"It's a bachelor-night thing. Remember?"

He scrubbed a hand over his face. "Why did I agree to all this?"

Grace sat down in the chair next to him. "I know. It's a big ask, but you don't know how much I appreciate it."

"I'm glad. I mean, you're not the only one at fault here. We both got incredibly drunk that night."

"Still, it meant a lot to have you there supporting me," she whispered.

He glanced over her at her sitting next to him, in that beautiful flowing summery dress, her silken blond hair blowing in the evening breeze, and all he wanted to do was pull her into his lap and hold her. Only he couldn't. No one would think anything of it here and it would just all be part of the act to her, but for him there was suddenly a very real yearning to hold her close. A yearning for intimacy which he hadn't felt in a long time.

It overwhelmed him. He wanted to tell her strong she was, stronger than she thought, and that he'd meant all of what he told Victor, but that would only lead somewhere he'd sworn never to go again. So he said nothing.

"Do want to head back to Vegas?" she asked.

"Yes." And instantly he felt relieved.

They both stood up and walked back into her parents' house to say good-night.

This was all a big ruse—Jonah knew that, and for better or for worse he'd promised her that he would keep it up. He just needed to learn to harden his emotions better, because if he didn't…

He couldn't bear the idea of loving and losing someone else and having to start all over in another new place.

Jonah offered to drive back to Las Vegas because when he was driving, he was able to block out all his indecisive thoughts and focus on the roads. It calmed him. The fact was he was enjoying his time with Grace more than he should've let himself. The night had been so awkward, but with her by his side, it had been easy to put on the facade—easy to pretend and play her husband. It kind of freaked him out that it had been so simple to slip into that role.

"You've gone quiet," Grace said. "You okay?"

"Just concentrating on the road. You should be used to me driving by now. I mean, I've driven before."

"I drive the rig," she teased.

Jonah heaved a big disdainful sigh. "True."

"Then what's up?"

"What do you mean?" he asked stiffly.

"You were like a totally different person with my family."

"It's all part of the act, right?"

"Right," she responded hesitantly, like she didn't believe him. "And now?"

"I'm fine. Just...worried about lying to your family. They're nice."

"I know, but trust me...this will be less stressful than telling them the truth."

"For them or you?" It was a blunt question. He knew that, but he was hoping for a truthful answer. Something he'd never gotten from Mona. He hoped Grace wouldn't lie to him.

"Both," she admitted. "Exes are complicated, as are rash decisions made when intoxicated."

He grunted. "Understatement of the year."

"You were married before, right?"

"I was. It ended badly. I was also cheated on. Trust is... It's hard to give."

Which was true.

When he'd come home after serving, he'd been so broken and had needed to heal.

***

"Mrs. Crandall? I'm Dr. Severn, your husband's therapist."

Jonah looked over at Mona, who only took his therapist's hand with a bit of prodding.

"Pleasure," she said through gritted teeth. "Not sure why I'm here. I don't have post-traumatic stress disorder."

Dr. Severn frowned for a moment. "I'm aware, Mrs. Crandall, but...you're Jonah's wife, and it's important that you're here. Your support is needed in this healing journey."

Mona nodded. "Okay. Medication dosing and such? Is that what you mean by support?"

"Well, yes, there are medications, but emotional support too," Dr. Severn responded.

"Okay," Mona replied quickly. "I thought he was over all of this PTSD when he took his discharge. I guess I don't understand what's happening or what more I can do. I mean, I already work two jobs since he went on disability."

"It's not about money, Mona," Jonah said quickly. "We need to repair our relationship. I need your emotional support. Can I trust you to make this work?"

Immediately he knew he'd offended her. Her body went ramrod straight, and she snapped her mouth shut. Out of the corner of his eye he saw Dr. Severn was looking back and forth at the both of them, clearly uncomfortable.

He hadn't meant to embarrass her, but her combative comments had put him on edge too.

"Of course," she replied tightly and plastered on a fake smile.

Jonah shook that painful memory away. The lie she'd told. She never had come to another therapy session. She'd never understood why the medication alone couldn't just fix it all so he could enlist again.

He'd foolishly thought Mona could help him out, but she hadn't wanted that burden. She'd always wanted the quick fix. As if medication alone was the solution to Jonah's problem. It did wonders for some and he promoted it to patients, but for him it just hadn't been enough alone.

The work he'd done in therapy to process his trauma had been long and difficult, but he'd been determined to stick to it because he'd been so invested in saving their marriage. Mona just hadn't wanted it like he had. She hadn't been willing to fight for him, for them. She didn't want to put in the effort.

He'd been a fool for wanting to save them so badly. All because he thought love was enough.

"That's it exactly," Grace said, interrupting his brooding. "Trust. I trusted Victor with my whole being, with my soul, but the fact that he cheated on me and everyone but me knew…it was humiliating."

"Did your family know? I mean, it's kind of crappy of them to be so okay with him after hurting you."

"No. I didn't tell them why it ended. I was so ashamed. They had to help me so much when I was a kid..." Grace trailed off and covered her mouth with her hand, like she was physically trying to stop herself from saying more. "They think I ended it. Maybe Travis knows, but I don't think so."

"I think you should tell them. They care about you."

"None of that matters now. I don't want to cause further rifts or friction leading up to Melanie's big day. It's going to be bad enough when this ends."

Jonah nodded. He understood that. But if Travis did know about his best friend doing that to Grace—his future sister-in-law—and saw no problem with it, well, who was to say Travis wouldn't do the same to Melanie?

Though Jonah prided himself on being a good judge of character, and Travis didn't seem like the type of person to do that. From the brief time he'd spent with them tonight, it seemed like Travis genuinely cared for Melanie. There was tenderness, respect, love. All the things Jonah wished he'd had with Mona back then but it was now clear he hadn't.

He secretly wanted all that still, but he didn't

know how to reach out and take it without the fear of being hurt.

The same way Grace had been hurt by Victor. Wouldn't she *want* to talk to her family about it? One thing Jonah had learned working through his PTSD was that you had to share and be more open. Bottling things up was never good.

Of course, he was one to talk.

But then, it was about opening up to the right people. And if you couldn't speak to your family, then something was wrong.

She must have her reasons.

Only those reasons, whatever they were, were not his concern. He had a part to play, and getting involved emotionally was not part of the deal.

"You can see the Strip," Grace remarked, changing the subject.

"Yeah, you can. I've never seen it from over here. It's nice."

All the brilliant lights illuminated the night sky. The *Welcome to Nevada* sign was big and bold as they crossed over the state line and left Utah behind.

"I'm ready to be home," she murmured, resting her head against the window.

"Yeah. I'm tired too." He was looking forward to tonight because he had a steady place to stay for a month. Not a short-term rental where he constantly had to move around. Grace's place was a nice condo, close to work, in a quiet residential neighborhood, and he was looking forward to staying put for a short time.

He just had to be careful. They might've been man and wife legally, but that was only a fragile piece of paper.

He couldn't let her in. This was all temporary. He couldn't get wrapped up in her life.

There was an expiration date on this marriage, and if he wanted to keep working with her afterward, it all had to stay professional. No matter how tempting she was.

CHAPTER FIVE

It was a thousand percent awkward when they got back to Grace's place after the family dinner in St. George. Jonah might've had a great stage presence when it came to her family, but much like when they were at work, he was a bit more withdrawn and quiet in private.

Normally when he was like this they were busy and it wouldn't bother her or faze her. Now it did. Probably because, thanks to her impulsiveness, they were stuck in this lie together.

Stop taking all the blame.

And that was the crux of the matter. She was putting it all on herself, like she usually did.

Jonah followed her up the stairs, and she spun around to say good-night, like they were on a date or something. Then she remembered he'd moved in.

"What?" he asked.

"I forgot you lived here."

A smile played on his lips. "Well, you invited me to move in."

"I did not," she gasped. "I believe it was your suggestion."

He grinned. "I guess it was."

"Still, I just forgot." She unlocked the door, swearing at herself inwardly for being such a weirdo. She unlocked the door, and he followed her in, shutting the door behind him, locking it.

"I want you to have my bed."

His eyes widened. "Your…what?"

"Not sharing," she said quickly. "I want you to have my bed. I know you said…"

Jonah held up his hand. "Grace, it's fine. I'm perfectly comfortable on the couch."

"You're sure?"

"Positive. I think I'm going to make use of the pool and go for a swim first."

Her stomach churned just at that thought. "Oh?"

"You okay with that?"

"Of course. Why wouldn't I be?"

"Do you ever use the pool?"

"No," she responded quickly. "I don't swim."

"What if I teach you?"

"No." She shook her head.

"Sure, but if you ever change your mind."

"I'd rather ride the motorcycle."

He cocked an eyebrow. "Well, that can be arranged."

"No helmet." She was really getting herself into somewhat of a pickle tonight.

Jonah didn't say anything else, and they just stood there, staring at each other.

"Well, I'll leave you to your swim." Grace backed away and retreated to her room.

She didn't want this to get any weirder than it already had. Not that the weirdness was a surprise. Awkward situations seemed to be her specialty a lot of the time, and getting drunk with a coworker and marrying him was definitely the epitome of that. How could it not be?

She heard the sound of the condo door shutting and relaxed a bit, taking the opportunity to get ready for bed.

When she glanced out her bedroom window, she could see Jonah was swimming laps, and truth be told, she was a bit envious of his ability to do that so easily. Something most people could do, but not her. There was a part of her that couldn't help but admire his strong body gliding through the crystal-blue water.

He was so handsome.

He's off-limits.

She shook her head in disgust at herself for lusting after him.

Again.

She was pretty sure this was also one of the reasons they'd ended up married. Why did she have to do something so foolish? Another stupid choice, just like the one she'd made as a kid that had led to her costly hospitalization. And, as her sister always liked to remind her, had taken up so much of their parents' attention.

As she sat there mulling and stewing about it, she heard the door open. Then it closed and there was a click of the lock, followed by Jonah puttering around her condo.

She turned out the lights. Tomorrow would be a new day. They'd both vowed to try and work together. She'd promised Jonah that, and she had to make it work. When all was said and done, he was a good partner.

The one good thing about living with your partner was that you both could leave for work at the same time. At least that was the positive spin that Grace was trying to put on the entire situation as she got used to having Jonah underfoot.

Actually, it wasn't bad having him around. She felt guilty that he'd been sleeping on her couch for the last couple of days, but he said he didn't mind it at all and that her couch was comfortable.

Still, he should've been the one to take the bed.

He was doing her a huge favor.

They'd had a couple of days off before their next shift, and they'd fallen into a sort of routine, just like they did at work. She'd get up, and he would be outside swimming laps. They would often share a meal, but it was always quiet. It didn't bother her, the silence. They ate their lunch together like that, and to her it was comfortable.

If anything, there was a little bit more conversation at dinner, just a touch. She kind of enjoyed it.

It was cozy, and it was freaking her out at how easy it was to be around him. She couldn't honestly recall ever being this comfortable with Victor in the beginning of their relationship.

You're not in a relationship with Jonah. Remember?

Now came the true test of this whole fandangle situation. They would have to go into work and deal with their coworkers—who, judging by a flurry of text messages both she and Jonah had received, were completely shocked that they had gotten married, because both of them had been so vocal about not wanting to get involved with anyone ever again. The only people who weren't surprised were the ones who'd been there. Like John, who had been their wedding videographer—something he was bragging about apparently.

Nothing stayed secret for long.

Grace took a deep breath and tucked her uniform shirt into her work pants and headed out into the other room. The moment she opened her bedroom door, she could smell coffee. It smiled like heaven, and her stomach rumbled in appreciation. She made her way into the kitchen.

"Good morning, partner," she greeted brightly.

"Want a cup?" Jonah asked.

"You never have to ask me." She took the mug

from him and breathed in the rich, deep scent that she loved so much. "Thanks for this."

"I figured we'd both need liquid courage heading into work today. We're going to be bombarded." He pursed his lips together. "Not looking forward to it."

"I know. Me neither."

"At least we're not going to get fired for it."

She nodded. "No, there's no policy on spouses working together. For now. As long as our personal feelings don't interfere with the job, we should be fine."

A strange expression crossed his face. "Right."

"You don't seem convinced."

"Honestly, I have a hard time working with people I'm friends with." His voice was tight and he had this far-off expression. She wondered what was wrong but knew she probably wouldn't find out. He didn't open up very often.

She cocked an eyebrow. "At least you're admitting we're friends now."

Jonah grinned, a dimple forming in his cheek. "Well, of course. We're married, and that's a good basis for marriage, right? Friendship?"

"Yes. I suppose so." She finished off her coffee. "I suppose we should arrive together. I mean, it would look weird if we traveled separately."

"Are you telling me you want to jump on the back of my bike?"

Adrenaline rushed through her as she pictured

Jonah between her thighs, her arms wrapped around his waist, holding on to him, her body pressed against his and the rumble of an engine beneath her. She had been fantasizing about it since she learned he rode a motorcycle. On Sunday he'd gone to his storage unit to get it and go for a drive. She thought he'd taken it back.

Apparently not.

"Don't you usually walk? I thought you didn't ride your bike?"

"I don't, but I forgot to take it back after my ride yesterday. So what do you say?"

"I could jump on the back of your bike." And she hoped her voice didn't break as she said it. "But we had this conversation before—I don't have a helmet."

"I've got you a helmet." He nodded to the direction of the front door and she saw the pink-and-black helmet. It definitely wasn't a spare one that he'd had lying around, which meant he'd gone out and gotten it for her. A pink one at that—her favorite color. He must have been inspired by the streak in her hair.

"You bought that for me?" She sat down her mug and picked it up, absolutely stunned.

"Yeah, I was out yesterday wandering around and saw a used-motorbike store. It was on sale, and I figured we could take some rides around the desert. I've always wanted to go to the Hoover

Dam and Lake Mead. You've lived here for some time. You could show me."

Her stomach clenched. The dam was so high and the water moved so fast. And while Lake Mead was gorgeous to look at from afar, she had no desire to get up close and personal with it. She avoided bodies of water, deep water, fast water at all costs.

"There's also the red rocks," she offered. "Great rock climbing."

She wasn't fond of heights either, but she could deal with that over water any day.

"That sounds like a plan. You ready to go to work and get this day over with?" he asked.

"Yes." She grabbed her bag and slung it over her shoulder, grabbing her helmet. Jonah followed her out, and she locked it behind them. She could see his motorcycle parked in her second parking spot, and her stomach did a little flip of nervousness and excitement.

She was pretty sure her aunt Gert or her mom would completely freak out knowing that she was on the back of what they liked to call a "death machine," but she was so excited to try it, and it was only a short drive to the firehouse.

Once upon a time she'd used to be a lot more adventurous and fun loving, but that was before her breakup with Victor. Then she'd sort of retreated a bit into herself, even when she was with him. She'd been so head over heels with him, and it all seemed so perfect. He had to impress the board of directors to further his career, so she'd tried to be the perfect girlfriend.

Now, looking back, that was what she regretted the most—hiding herself.

If being with someone meant she had to change to fit their ideal, she didn't want it. It just didn't appeal to her.

"You okay with this?" Jonah asked as he slung one leg over the seat and put on his helmet. He seemed a bit nervous too. Grace knew it took a great deal of trust to have someone ride on the back of a bike with you. Maybe he was relaxing around her just a bit.

She nodded confidently. "Yeah, I am."

She climbed on behind him, his body so close it made her pulse race as she gingerly wrapped her arms around his hard, muscular chest and tucked herself against him. He started the engine, the motor rumbling beneath her as he revved it.

"Hold on," he said over his shoulder as he slowly pulled out of the parking lot and onto the Summerlin streets. She closed her eyes and gripped him tight; she knew he was laughing by the way his body moved under her arms, but with her helmet on she couldn't hear a thing over the sound of the wind the motorcycle's engine.

Eventually, she opened her eyes and was able to enjoy the scenery of their suburb going by. The beauty of the ochre-colored mountains, the subtle wave of the palm trees lining the boulevard and the bright blue sunny sky.

It reminded her why she loved living in the desert. Her favorite moment was in the morning, when there was no heat to the sun and everything was bright, crisp and new. No dust devils or tumbleweed. Just peace. She wanted to savor that moment a little longer before they got to work and their shift started, because if there was one thing she had learned about being a paramedic in Las Vegas, there was never a day off.

They pulled into the parking lot of the fire station and parked around back. There were several of their coworkers milling about when Jonah parked the bike. The knot in the pit of Grace's stomach grew as she slowly slid off the bike and realized they had to face the music.

Jonah was grinning as he got off. "You okay?"

"Why are you asking me that?"

"Oh, maybe because of the death grip you had on my nipples," he whined, jokingly rubbing his shirt over his chest. "Seriously, did you have to give me a purple nurple?"

She was surprised at his joking, and she kind of liked it. When he'd been around her family, he was like that—affable, jovial, social and charming. Someone she rarely saw when they were alone.

Maybe the mask is coming back because we're at work?

But she shook that thought away.

"I didn't!" Then she giggled. "Okay, maybe I was a little nervous. You drive fast."

"I like it fast, but I can always guarantee that it's a pleasurable ride." He winked and sauntered off, leaving her stunned.

Well, she'd walked right into that one. She stood there for a few more moments, watching him as he was surrounded by their coworkers, who were all obviously dying to know the details about their wedding.

Grace took a deep breath and walked into the fray. There was no better time than now to rip the bandage off the proverbial wound.

Grace rubbed her temple, hoping the headache would subside. She was very glad to be in the rig and out on patrol and away from all the questions. She couldn't remember the last time she had been so bombarded with so many. It was overwhelming for her, but Jonah seemed to take it all in stride. Honestly, she thought maybe their coworkers were more shocked by the fact he was being so social than the news of the wedding itself.

"Thanks for letting me take the wheel this shift," Jonah said. "I like driving."

"Thanks for offering. My head was pounding by the time they were finished grilling us."

"They were definitely curious."

"That's putting it mildly," she teased. "And

thanks for answering the vast majority of questions. I was in shock. I don't usually get that much attention."

"I don't *like* that much attention," he admitted. "So much for keeping to myself."

They shared a smile. "I can see why we were paired together when you arrived," Grace said.

"Because we're antisocial?"

She laughed. "I think so."

"We're not mean per se."

"No. We just like to keep to ourselves." She enjoyed this teasing conversation. It was breezy.

"That backfired," he groused. A smile quirked on his lips.

"It was your suggestion to go out that night!"

"Sure. Blame me!"

They both laughed at the absurdity of the conversation.

"I will admit it's so easy to talk to you now. Why is that?"

His expression softened and he shrugged. "I suppose that's a good thing, seeing as we're married and all."

"Was that all it took to get you to open up?" she pondered out loud.

"I am trying to put myself out there."

"I appreciate that."

There was an awkward silence, and he sighed. "I don't want our working relationship to be ruined when this is all done."

And that was the truth to it all. There was a finality to this whole marriage, and then she'd go back to her regular life, which didn't seem that appealing at the moment.

"Right," she agreed quietly. "I filed a petition online. It's going to take a month. I'm sorry about that, but since we were..."

Grace couldn't even bring herself to say the words, which was silly because she was an adult and had done the horizontal mambo before. Although in this case, foggy memories told her they'd spent some of their time together vertical and sideways too. And thinking about those hazy flashes made her blood crackle with want. A coil of pleasure and anticipation wound tightly deep in her belly, seeking release.

Focus, Grace!

"You mean since we had sex?" Jonah said, finishing off her sentence.

Her cheeks flushed. "Right."

"You know what? It was worth it."

Her heart skipped a beat as their gazes locked across the rig. She wanted to tell him she agreed, because as the days went on from their encounter, she was remembering more and more of their night together—that amazing, magical, pleasure-filled night. But before she could reminisce with him, a call came over the radio from dispatch.

"Rig three, we have a code four, color orange.

Male complaining of abdominal pains post-surgery. Sending you the address," dispatch stated.

"Roger that. En route," Jonah responded as the address popped up on the screen. Grace flicked on the lights and siren as Jonah navigated the streets to get to the location. She gripped the door and relaxed as the ambulance whizzed through Vegas streets.

It didn't take them too long to reach the address. Grace shut out everything else as Jonah and she worked seamlessly together, getting their gear and making their way to the patient's house.

Just like at her parents' place there was a crowd gathered outside, but the man they were going to assess was inside, so they wouldn't have an audience while they worked. A middle-aged woman holding a phone was waiting at the door.

"Manuel Lopez?" Grace questioned.

"I'm his wife. I called because Manuel had gallbladder surgery two days ago. He's had severe pain and hives. He can't keep anything down, and I don't drive."

"Show us," Jonah said gently.

Mrs. Lopez nodded, and they carried the stretcher up over the front steps into the house. The patient, Manuel, was lying in bed and appeared jaundiced. Grace could see the yellowing of his skin from the doorway, even in the dim lighting.

If nothing else was wrong, that right there was a reason to go to the hospital.

"Mr. Lopez? I'm a paramedic. Grace Landon. And this is my partner, Jonah. We're here to help you."

Mr. Lopez nodded. "The pain—it's not from the incisions."

"When did you have surgery?" Grace asked, pulling on her gloves.

"Three days ago," Manuel stated, wincing.

"Mind if we check the incision sites?" Jonah asked.

Manuel nodded, lifting his shirt. "Go ahead."

Jonah palpated around the incision sites as Grace assessed the jaundice in Mr. Lopez's eyes.

"No redness or swelling at the incision sites, but he does have some swelling and petechiae," Jonah remarked.

"Jaundice too." Grace took the patient's temperature. "Fever as well."

Jonah nodded. "We're going to take you to the hospital to have you checked. Where was your surgery performed?"

"Vegas Central," Mrs. Lopez answered. "I've called his surgeon's office."

"Good." Grace prepared the intravenous line to get some medication and fluid into Manuel for the transport. It also gave them easy access in case something happened on the way to the hospital.

"We'll get you there safely, Mr. Lopez," Jonah reassured as they worked side by side together.

That was the thing she liked about working with Jonah. Neither of them had to say anything. It was like they knew what each other was thinking and were on the same page. It made him a good partner, and that made her a little sad.

Had she royally messed up their good working partnership? When this all ended would she lose the best partner she'd ever had?

She wasn't sure, but she wouldn't let her mind get bogged down with that.

Not right now.

They got Manuel prepped, loaded into the ambulance and safely delivered to Vegas Central, and thankfully she didn't have any run-ins with Victor. They were able to hand off Mr. Lopez to the doctor who had done his surgery.

As she and Jonah wheeled their empty gurney out to their rig, he let out a soft grunt as they loaded up the equipment.

"You okay?" she asked.

"Yep. Just hungry. Lunch break?"

Grace checked her watch. "I suppose so."

"Great. I know an awesome food truck on our route."

"Food truck?"

"I didn't pack a lunch today, did you?"

"No, I guess I didn't."

"Food truck it is, then." He locked the back door. "I'll drive, and you can finish the report."

She laughed out loud. "So that's the real reason you're offering to take me out for lunch—to get out of paperwork."

Jonah winked. For the most part he was quiet, but she liked this other side to him, the little glimmers she was getting to see. They climbed back into the ambulance and belted up as they left the ambulance bay of Vegas Central.

"I also have an ulterior motive to this food truck lunch," he said.

"An ulterior motive?"

"Well, we have to book a tee time for ourselves."

"Oh, golf. Right."

"Travis texted me. It's on Friday, and I have no idea what I'm doing." He frowned again, his lips a tight line. "Ugh. I hate this."

"What?"

"Golf—and with strangers particularly."

Grace shook her head. "You could back out."

"What, and let your father down?"

"Does it matter? I mean, a month from now this will be all over."

"I know, but I don't like letting people down and we'll still be married by your sister's wedding date. I guess I should try, keep up the pretense."

A pang of guilt hit her. He was doing so much for her, and he was so nice. This whole thing was absolutely her fault because she'd panicked and was embarrassed about having broadcasted her drunken wedding nuptials.

This wasn't her usual modus operandi but just further proved to her the point that there really wasn't such a thing as a happily-ever-after.

No fairy-tale love.

No romance.

She'd learned her lesson.

Jonah had been going to buy Grace lunch, but she insisted on buying as he'd driven her to work and to the food truck. That was the excuse she gave him, but he had a hunch she was feeling guilty about this whole fake-marriage thing.

She wasn't totally at fault. He'd agreed to it as well. Honestly, he was experiencing a bit of guilt too because he was enjoying spending time with her a little too much, and he knew Grace didn't want a relationship with someone she worked with. It was hard not to think about that when she'd climbed on the back of his bike this morning, clinging to him. It had made him think about her in his arms. It had felt so right.

When he'd originally bought that helmet, for one moment he'd thought he was wasting his money because he'd never believed she'd actually go for a ride with him. He was glad she'd said yes, but then he'd started to worry about keeping her safe on the back of his bike.

He'd seen enough motorcycle accidents in his years.

Yet she'd trusted him, and it felt good that she did. Mona never had. She'd hated his bike.

That trust was something else he liked about Grace. He was so attracted to her, even more so now that they'd spent more time together.

If they didn't have to work, he'd have been tempted to keep on driving, maybe head up to Lake Tahoe and woo her in a cabin. He had a friend who was a surgeon in Vegas, Dr. Nick Rousseau, who had a cabin up near Tahoe.

And he knew for a fact Nick and his wife, Dr. Jennifer Mills, weren't using it at the moment, as they were waiting on the arrival of another baby.

He could totally take Grace there. More importantly, he wanted to.

Get your head on straight. She's your partner, not your wife!

Jonah had to push all those romantic notions to the side. That wasn't in his plan. Only it was easy to forget that when he looked at her.

Especially now as they sat on picnic table, outside their rig on the side of a desert highway eating fries and gourmet hot dogs from a food truck, like any couple would. It wasn't weird or awkward; it felt natural. Like they had done this one hundred times before.

Like it was supposed to be.

But he'd been duped by these emotions before, and it was hard not to think about that.

Grace isn't Mona.

Grace was someone he felt like maybe he could open up to.

"Oh, my gosh. These fries are amazing," Grace remarked, dipping another one into a big blob of ketchup.

"Told you."

"Where did you find this food truck?"

"When I was moving to Vegas. There's a cool fifties diner between here and California too."

She smiled, her mouth full of fries. It was adorable, kind of like a pink-haired chipmunk. "That would be fun."

"I'll make you a deal."

She cocked any eyebrow. "Is that what our marriage is all about? Deals?"

He laughed at her gentle ribbing. "Do you want to hear my idea or not?"

"Fine." There was a glow in her eyes, a mischievous glint he'd seen before. It had been that look she got on her face right before she suggested they get married. "Lay it on me, daddio."

"Daddio?" he asked.

"You were talking about a fifties diner, and I was just using the lingo."

"I suppose I was...uh...mammio."

Grace choked. "What?"

"Never mind," he groused. "Clearly I don't know old-timey lingo."

"You don't. And you're older than me," she ribbed.

"By seven years."

She snickered. "Old man."

"Well, this conversation is not going as I pictured."

Grace chuckled. "Sorry, sorry. I derailed you. What were you going to ask?"

"Never mind."

She rolled her eyes. "Come on. What were you saying?"

"My suggestion, or deal, was that you teach me to golf before Friday, and Saturday we'll take a bike ride out to that fifties diner."

"Do I have to dress up?"

"No."

"That's a shame."

Now he was intrigued. "Are you telling me you want to wear a poodle skirt?"

"No," she responded emphatically. "Look, you don't have to make a deal with me for me to teach you to golf."

"So you don't want to go to the diner?" he teased.

"I didn't say that."

"Well?"

She moved to sit next to him. "Sure. It's a deal. We could go golfing tomorrow night and the night after that, and then, if we survive Friday, we'll go to a diner sometime to celebrate."

"I can't learn golf in one night?"

"Uh...no."

"Damn," he muttered but then looked at her in growing awe, imagining her kicking ass on the golf course. There was so much about her he didn't know, but he wanted to learn more. She was vivacious and interesting. "Where did you learn to play?"

She wrinkled her nose. "The country club."

"That's the second time you've barely hid your contempt for the country club. What's with that?"

She sighed. "Well, my dad had to give up memberships for a while. My hospital bills were hefty after my accident. He missed it and rejoined a few years ago. I always felt bad."

"That wasn't your fault."

She gave a half shrug like she didn't believe him. "I don't know... It's so pretentious. Victor loved it. My dad and him bonded over it. It's just a reminder to me of a lot of failings."

"Your dad puts value on that?" he asked.

"No. I don't think so." She shrugged again. "It's all so superficial."

"Agreed, but at least you learned how to play golf."

She laughed and gave him a nudge with her shoulder, leaning against him. He could smell her clean scent, only this time he could also get a whiff of the malt vinegar and ketchup on her fries.

It was weird, but it reminded him of his dad, who had been British. Not so much the ketchup, but the malt vinegar. His mother would make homemade fries—or chips, as his dad called them—and he would douse them in salt and vinegar. If his dad could've had his way, he would've had them every day.

"You went really quiet," she remarked. "What're you thinking about?"

"My dad, actually."

"Oh?" said softly. "How many years ago did he pass?"

"Years ago, when I was overseas. He was a bit aloof, but he wasn't ever mean. My parents were in their mid-forties when I was born. Actually, Dad was closer to fifty."

All of it came rolling off his tongue so easily. It felt natural to talk about them with her. He hadn't spoken about them in so long.

Grace's eyes widened. "Wow."

He nodded in the direction of her fries. "You put malt vinegar on there, and it reminded me of him. He was British. He met an American girl, moved to California."

She smiled. "Well, I'm glad the smell isn't making you want to retch and gave you a happy recollection."

"Yeah, I'm glad too." And he let that pleasant

little memory percolate for a few more moments in his mind as the cars from the highway whizzed by them. It was always easier to lock them all away so he could work, but it was nice to have that reminder of his dad.

Almost like a visit from his father, letting him know he was here.

Still.

For a moment Jonah was less lonely.

Grace sighed and finished her fries. "I guess lunch break is over."

"I suppose." He collected up the trash from his lunch and took it over to the garbage receptacle, and Grace followed him. They sanitized their hands and headed back to the ambulance to continue their shift.

There had never really been a moment like that that he shared with Mona. Not that he could think of. When he'd come home from duty, there had been things he wanted to talk about with her so that he could move on and heal, but she'd never wanted to hear it.

Or maybe she couldn't hear it. So he'd spent so much time keeping things to himself.

Back then it was so much simpler that way, but when he was around Grace it was different.

He could be himself and he didn't have to lock things away.

CHAPTER SIX

A couple days later

"YOU KNOW...MAYBE I should go with you on Friday." Grace winced as Jonah took another swing once again and missed the ball. It was almost comical, and she was pretty sure she had never seen play this bad in real life. He was trying though—she had to credit him with that.

She'd decided before she booked a tee time for an actual game that maybe it was best they try the driving range first. Boy, was she glad she had. He had the swing and the power; it was just the connecting part he seemed to be struggling with.

"Seriously?" He grunted staring at the ball in frustration. "I can play hockey."

She laughed to herself. "A puck is bigger."

"I know. I was making a joke about a movie—the golfer who was a hockey player."

She was painfully aware of that movie now. Since their lunch at the food truck, their own dinners at home had gotten more chatty. And then that had morphed into watching movies at night. They took turns to choose, and so far it was working.

Even if Jonah's movie choices were terrible.

"And that's why that was a movie. A far-fetched movie. A lot of pro hockey players do play golf, but I'm not sure that should be your argument on why *you* should be able to play golf."

"So you're not going to tell me it's all in the hips?" Jonah winked and lined up again.

"Well, it is in the hips and your..." She trailed off as he swung, a whooshing sound slicing through the air, but the ball was remained on the tee. "It's your follow-through."

He grunted. "What follow-through?"

"Line it up again." She stood behind him, slipping her arms over his, her hips pressed against his backside, and she was suddenly very aware at how close she was to him.

Just like when she'd been pressed up against him on the bike. Her hands were so small over his tanned, muscular forearms, and all she could hear was the thundering of her pulse between her ears.

Galloping would be the correct word to describe it, and she fought the urge to caress his arms, because she remembered what it felt like to run her hands over his skin. The more time they spent together, the more she thought about it.

"Don't take your eyes off the target," she said, finally finding her voice. She imitated the swing behind him, guiding his hands as they grasped the club.

"Okay," he responded.

Grace stepped away quickly, hugging herself and trying to shake away the remnants of her arousal from being so close to him again, because she did want him. She wanted to be close to him, even though he was off-limits.

Jonah took a swing, and this time there was contact, a definite thwack as the driver met the golf ball, and it sailed up and over the green toward the big black net at the end of the range.

His eyes widened, and he raised up his arms, like a hockey player scoring a goal. "See that?"

Grace grinned, enjoying his enthusiasm. "Great job. Now you have to do it again. Over and over until this bucket of balls is gone."

"Are you insinuating that it was a fluke shot?"

"Maybe," she hinted with a wicked smile.

Jonah frowned. "I'll show you."

She watched as he placed a new ball on the tee and lined up his shot, hitting the ball again.

"Woo-hoo! See that? I've got this."

His confidence was absolutely adorable. As she got to know him she was beginning to see little fragments of it. Like he was feeling safe with her. And at least he could now hit the ball and wouldn't look like a train wreck out on the course with her father, Travis and Victor. However, she'd feel so much better if she went golfing with them, but usually golf was a party of four or six, not five, and how would that look to everyone? Like she was keeping tabs on him or something. So she'd just have to make sure she got Jonah up to speed on the game.

It was nice he was willing to play along with this, even when it was all fake.

"Uh-oh."

"What?" Grace asked, quickly looking over her shoulder.

"You're worrying your bottom lip and wringing your hands together. What're you thinking about?"

"Nothing."

Jonah raised an eyebrow. "Sure."

"Fine. I was thinking how you really don't have to do this."

"Do what?" He took another swing, driving the ball farther this time. "Be excellent at golf?"

She rolled her eyes. "This is one aspect of the game."

"I know. So what's eating at you?"

"You're going to a lot of trouble to help me perpetrate this...this lie."

"I don't mind, Grace. We're friends, right?"

"We're partners," she teased.

"Ouch." He winced. "Right in the feels."

"You are incorrigible. What happened to that quiet partner I used to have?"

"I've adjusted." He swung again, hitting the

last ball out of the bucket they'd bought. He set his driver back in the bag, came over to her and rested his hands on her shoulders. "Look, we both made rash decisions that night. Stop shouldering the blame for it all."

"Still…"

"No. There's no *but*. Grace, you're a good partner and I like spending time with you."

Her heart fluttered, but it also terrified her that this was going so fast. From partners to friends… and then where? She didn't want to date someone from work. She couldn't have more with him.

She couldn't accept more.

"I'll concede we're friends. And as a friend, I think I need to buy you a congratulatory ice cream to celebrate your success."

"That I will accept." Jonah picked up the rented clubs, and they headed back to return them then made their way to the car. This time it was up to Grace to pick a spot for ice cream, and she knew a perfect little cafe in Summerlin which overlooked the mountains and a cute park where people walked their dogs and kids came to play. There was a pond and picnic tables, and best of all, it was quieter than trying to find a place on the Strip.

Once they got to the park and ordered their ice cream, they took a walk and found a secluded bench by the pond to watch the ducks.

"So, since we're friends you won't mind me asking you some questions," Grace said.

"Sure," he said, nodding his head.

"How can a man who served in the Marines not hit a target?"

Jonah chirped gleefully. "Well, that's different. Also, I was a medic."

"You still needed to have good aim."

"Yes, but there was no swinging involved." He frowned.

"What're you thinking about?" she asked gently.

"Nothing."

"Hey, friends, right?"

Jonah frowned and shrugged. "I thought the Marines would be good. My best friend, Justin, and I joined up and…"

Immediately she could tell he was upset, that it was hard for him to talk about. Just like she struggled to speak about her own experience almost drowning as a child and how she'd been duped by Victor. Jonah was hedging, and she wondered if it had something to do with trust.

And she understood that.

It was hard to give.

They were friends, and she wanted to give him that support. She wanted to get to know him. They were in this situation together, and she wanted to be there for him, like he was supporting her.

"And?" she asked quietly.

"He was killed." Jonah swallowed hard and then stared at the half-empty cup of ice cream in his hands. "Killed in the line of duty. He died right in my arms."

Seeing the pain etched across his face made her feel that dejection just as keenly. It was always hard losing a patient, but to have your best friend die in your arms... She couldn't imagine it.

That look on Jonah's face was the same one her mother would get face when she'd talk about Grace's drowning incident. Grace always felt bad about it, that she had caused her mother than much pain.

And it had been her own fault for not listening to her parents and being defiant and going into the pool without supervision.

"Oh, my gosh. I'm so sorry."

He nodded. "I've put a lot of effort into working through that."

"I'm sure."

"Therapy, medication. Still..." He trailed off.

"It's hard." She admired him for doing the work. She was envious. Maybe she could confront her own fears. Maybe Jonah could help. Only she didn't know how to ask. "So you became a paramedic because you were a medic?"

"It's why I love being a paramedic. Once I was discharged, I worked so hard to become a first responder, to get to this level, because I wanted to save lives. Yeah, I'd been a medic, but I wanted to do more because I really didn't want people to experience the pain that I felt. It came at a price though. My first wife didn't understand what I was going through, and honestly, the more I think about it now, she really didn't want to understand it."

Grace nodded. "I'm sorry that happened to you. And you should be proud of all you've accomplished."

"You should too," Jonah said fiercely.

"Really?" she responded gruffly. "I haven't faced my fear."

"Oh, I think you do."

"How so?"

"Well, you do save people in drowning incidents. I mean, what made you want to be a paramedic?"

No one had really asked her that before. "My near drowning when I was a kid is why I got into this profession. It was a woman who saved my life. I've never forgotten her. She was my hero, and I wanted to be strong and badass just like her. I wanted to be first on the scene."

What she didn't say was that the more lives she saved, the fewer mothers had to be sad. Like she could somehow atone for putting her parents through that. She was sparing pain, saving somebody's loved one. Every patient belonged to someone.

Their gazes locked across the bench, and they

shared a smile. Grace melted. She'd never really talked about Liz, the paramedic who saved her life before. How she idolized her and wanted to be like her, because in her mind Liz was a superhero. Grace had only met her once after the accident, when she was finally released from the hospital. And she never forgot that moment. She carried it with her.

And she hoped that she was half the kind of person that Liz was to her.

"You are badass," Jonah said, looking away and scooping up a spoonful of his ice cream.

"Oh?"

"Come on. When you're out there in an emergency situation you have this calm demeanor and nothing fazes you."

"Water does."

Jonah shrugged. "Yeah, but you continue to work hard to save lives."

"Thanks. I'm glad you're my partner. Honestly, I couldn't pick a better one. Even if you were a bit quiet in the beginning." She smiled slyly. "I sometimes miss that quieter version of you."

He laughed. "I guess there's no going back now."

"No, but I do worry about the future. Things have changed."

Jonah nodded quietly and finished the rest of his ice cream. "I do too. I don't want things to change too much when we finally get our divorce or annulment, whatever you want to call it. We're not strangers, but what we have now is nice."

"I don't want that either. It was bad enough dating a surgeon that I have to deal with on a semi-regular basis. I really don't want it to get awkward with you."

"It won't," he responded.

"How can you be so sure?"

He held up his hand, pinky up. "Let's pinky swear. We won't let any kind of personal emotion at the end of this fake marriage stop us from being friends or partners."

Grace nodded and hooked her pinky around his. "Pinky swear."

"Good."

She nodded, because it was the truth. She wanted to stay friends with him after this was all said and done. She didn't want to ruin what they already had because of a drunken night.

She was completely ignoring the other part of her, the part she was keeping buried deep down that wanted to explore more with Jonah.

The part that wanted that happy ending.

The part that still believed in all that.

Once they got back to Grace's condo, Jonah quickly changed and went down to swim some laps in the pool. Bringing up Justin and talking a little about his PTSD had made his anxiety spike. When he'd been discharged and trying to move forward with his life, he'd worked so hard with therapists to deal with the unbelievable nightmare of having his best friend die in his arms and the rejection that came from his ex-wife.

He didn't like to talk about it much.

Grace was the first person in Vegas that he'd actually admitted it to. Grace was the first person to whom he'd actually said Justin's name out loud. It had been so long since he'd talked about his best friend with someone who hadn't known him.

It had been good to let it all out, but he was a bit nervous about sharing that moment with her. It was hard being vulnerable with her, and while he didn't regret it, he really needed to blow off some steam away from her.

Swimming was a great exercise. Even though it was blistering hot during the day, it was cold at night when the desert got dark, and he really liked swimming in the heated pool then, even with the tendrils of steam curling off the surface.

He swam a few laps to work off that energy and then got out, wrapping his towel around his waist, running barefoot up the stairs to Grace's condo. He unlocked the door and headed inside. The door to her bedroom was shut, and she had said that she was going to bed. That sounded like a good idea to him. Though a very loud, demanding piece of his mind wished he could climb into bed with her and hold her.

If he was being honest, he wanted to do more than just hold her.

Don't think like that.

He shook all those thoughts from his mind and stepped into the bathroom to have a quick shower. A cold one.

When he got out, he realized he'd forgotten his jogging pants that he usually wore when he went to sleep. He cursed under his breath at his forgetfulness, wrapped a towel round his waist and dashed out. When he went to grab the joggers from where they were folded on the end of the couch, he let the towel drop to the floor and heard a gasp from behind.

He spun around and saw Grace standing there, a glass of milk in her hand, her eyes wide and a pink tinge on her supple cheeks. Their gazes locked, and all he could do was just stand there, staring at her in her oversized T-shirt. The hem of the shirt brushed the tops of her tanned thighs, so he got a full view of those long, firm legs. He wanted to run his hands over them. Hell, he wanted to run those hands higher.

She cleared her throat and looked away quickly. He grabbed the towel off the floor to cover himself back up.

"Sorry—I thought you were in bed," he apologized.

"No need to apologize. I couldn't sleep." She

held up her milk but wouldn't look him in the eye. "Were you taking a shower?"

"Done."

"I can see that," she whispered, tucking her hair behind her ear.

Make a joke. Anything to ease the tension.

"Well, we had a pretty good run. Living together for a whole week and we've just now had our first naked interlude."

It was the goofiest joke and completely cringe-worthy. He regretted it instantly, and if he could hide, he would.

Grace laughed and sputtered. "A what?"

"Naked encounter, I mean." He winked, hoping it melted the tension.

She snort-laughed. "*Naked interlude* sounds like a one of those strip clubs."

"It does." He smiled. "I hope this won't make things weird between us."

"This? No, I think this is not as weird as our wedding. Awkward, yes, but not enough to scare me away."

"Good."

This time she was looking him in the eye, but there was still that twinkle, that sparkle that made his heart beat a little beat faster. He was a sucker for her soft, tender glances. He could get lost in her gaze if he wanted to, and he very much did want to.

"Well, I better get to bed" Grace said. "We

have work, and I booked us a tee time for an actual game after our shift."

"A game?"

"You have to be ready for Friday, and then we're having dinner with my family in St. George on Saturday. A pre-wedding thing. My mom didn't explain it well in her text."

"It sounds good." He was lying, and he knew Grace knew that, because she was smirking.

"Oh, it'll be fun," she replied sardonically.

"Hopefully Aunt Gert has mastered the mascara this week." Just another joke to dispel the awkwardness.

Grace laughed loudly, holding her belly. He noticed the oversized shirt rode up, and he caught a sight of pink lacy underwear, making his pulse pound. He tried to look away.

"Doubtful. Aunt Gert always does lay it on thick. Thank you for not staring at it."

"It was hard not to. It was like orbs or planetoids of mascara. Things were orbiting the tips of her lashes."

"You're awful."

"Just easing the tension." He winked.

"Good night, Jonah."

"Good night, Grace."

He watched her as she walked away, back into her room. She was pulling at the back hem of her T-shirt in an attempt to cover up the delicious curve of her bottom. It was cute that she tried, though he still got a tempting eyeful. He exhaled and stared at the couch, wishing he was back in her bed.

The sleeping arrangements hadn't really been bothering him.

Until now.

Maybe he needed a glass of warm milk too. Maybe that would help him sleep, but he seriously doubted it.

CHAPTER SEVEN

THE WEEK SEEMED to drag on until the dreaded G-Day for Jonah.

Also known as Golf Day.

The game wasn't bad; he just wasn't any good at it. Grace had tried to show him several times. They'd even played a whole round of mini golf. It was just no use. He'd come to the foregone conclusion that he'd never be any good at it, and that was mostly fine by him. Did he want to impress Grace's father? Yes, but then he had to ask himself why. Grace wasn't really Jonah's, so what her dad thought of him didn't particularly matter in the long run.

Except it did.

It surprised him that he wanted to be the best fake son-in-law he could be. Which was kind of pathetic when he really thought about it.

He liked Grace, and from what he had seen of her family, he liked them too. They were loud and eager to be in her business, but they genuinely seemed to care. At first he'd really dreaded it, but he had spoken to Grace's little brother a couple of times since the family dinner, and her mother too.

It was nice to be invited to the pre-wedding stuff. It had been a long time since he felt like he belonged somewhere and with a family group. Grace was lucky that way, and he slightly envied her.

And if he admitted it to himself, he was going to miss it when this whole fake marriage was over. Part of him didn't want to let that feeling go.

Do you have to let it go? a little voice asked.

It shocked him for a moment, but he'd been mulling this over all week. It annoyed him that he was brooding on it, being vulnerable about that deep desire for more than solitude. He'd thought he'd learned his lesson, but being around Grace it was hard not to let those happy what-ifs trickle through his mind. And they were coming frequently.

Truth be told, he'd assumed the awkwardness of having slept with her would eventually catch up to them at work, but it hadn't. Grace was strong in herself and mature. It was a breath of fresh air compared to other women he knew.

"You ready?" Grace asked, interrupting his thoughts as she came out of her room. She was dressed in a white skort and a pink athletic shirt with a visor. Her hair was tied back, like she had it styled when they were at work. She was absolutely adorable, and he couldn't help but admire her muscular, shapely calves.

"You're dressed for golf," he said.

"I am. It seems Victor was called in for a patient, and Dad asked me to be the fourth. Is that okay?"

Jonah grinned. "Is my relief showing?"

He hadn't been looking forward to spending time with her ex; he saw enough of him when they took patients to the emergency department at Vegas Central. And now that Jonah was married to Grace, Victor had been weirder at work for sure. The energy was off-putting. Almost like Victor was jealous of him, which was childish seeing how Victor had chosen another over Grace. Then again, Jonah got the impression that Victor was the possessive, competitive type.

"Just a little bit," Grace chided. "It'll go great. I'm sure of it."

"You keep saying that," he teased.

"I know, but it's because I know it to be true."

"Well, do I look okay?" He held up his arms wide and slowly turned.

Grace cocked her head to one side, tapping her chin thoughtfully, studying him and making him sweat, thinking he'd got something wrong. "I think so. You're very dashing in your khakis and polo shirt."

"Dashing?"

She nodded. "Yes. You'll fit right in."

"Good. By the way, I quite like that word. *Dashing.*"

"I figured you would." She grabbed some of their gear, but they'd have to rent clubs at the course, because Jonah wasn't going to invest in something he wasn't going to play again.

"Come on, then. We better not be late for tee time, or my dad will be annoyed."

He didn't say anything, but he was struck by how Grace was so eager to please her family yet groaned when she was around them. It was almost like she thought she wasn't enough and needed to make up for it, when clearly that was not the case. She was more than enough. At least he thought so, and that fleeting little thought gave him pause.

The country club was a bit north of the condo and the Red Rock Canyon. As they drove out into the desert and mountains, it seemed a bit surreal that there were greens from the course and bodies of water sprawled out under the burning heat amid the browns and ochres that usually dominated the Nevada vista. As they turned down the long drive, the clubhouse looked a little bit like a modern-day adobe mirage, rising white out of the sands. He liked it quite a bit. It was out of place and yet fit in. Maybe a bit like him.

They parked and made their way to the check-in, where Rick and Travis were waiting. Jonah stood back as Grace greeted her dad and Travis.

"Sorry," she apologized. "Work ran late."

"Oh? Was it a hard day?" Rick asked, hugging his daughter.

"No. Just long."

"Jonah, good to see you," Rick greeted gruffly, turning to him. "It should be a great evening."

"It should. Thank you for inviting me, Mr. Landon," Jonah said, hoping that he sounded somewhat enthused by this whole prospect, because he wasn't.

"You can call me Rick instead of Mr. Landon. We're family."

Family. What a nice thought. Except they weren't. Not really. And Rick said it tightly, almost protectively, like he didn't quite believe it either. Not that Jonah blamed him at all. He knew all about trust.

Jonah nodded, and Grace's eyes were a bit wide with worry. Rightfully so. Not only did she have to worry about the fake marriage lie and hurting her family, but he knew, even if she didn't admit it, that his golf game was nil. And what should've been an enjoyable evening might end up a tedious slog.

Would Grace's father still let Jonah call him Rick after he saw how he played? Time would tell.

"We have two carts booked. We could pair up. I'll take Travis in mine, and you two newlyweds can take the other," Rick suggested.

"Sounds good, Dad," Grace responded. She

nodded, and Jonah trailed after her, dragging his feet a bit.

They found their assigned carts and got all their clubs and gear loaded. Rick and Travis took the lead golf cart, and Jonah and Grace had the one behind.

"Sorry you're stuck with me," he groused half-heartedly.

"This is better than it would have been."

"Why, because I suck?"

"Well…" She grinned deviously. "But also imagine making small talk with Victor." Grace shuddered. "At least I know how bad you are at the game. If he knew he'd tease you every time he saw you again."

"Right. Good point."

"Now I can tease you."

"Hey!" Jonah nudged her as she laughed. They followed behind Rick's cart to the first flag on the course. "So, any tips?"

Grace continued to giggle. "Well, think about connecting the ball when you go to take your swing."

"Why is that so funny?"

"It's not. I laugh when I'm nervous sometimes."

"And why are you nervous? You don't suck at golf," he groused.

"Getting you involved deeper with my family."

"Yes. That thought had crossed my mind.

Man, if your dad tolerates me now, he'll loathe me later."

"He doesn't just tolerate you."

"Oh, really?"

Grace worried at her bottom lip. "He's protective of us kids. He treated Victor the same. He treated Travis the same too. Would you like to leave?"

He wanted to say yes, but that wouldn't look good at all. "Well, we're here now. We've just got to play the part."

"Right. Of course."

He sensed a little disappointment in her voice. It was just for a moment though.

She rolled her shoulders and plastered on a determined expression. "As for your game, connect and keep your eyes when you follow through."

"Yes. I know."

"You're going to be okay."

"Uh-huh. Sure."

She shook her head as they pulled their golf cart up next to her father's. Travis was going to tee off first, as he was the bachelor for whom this evening was meant. He took his shot, and they watched at the ball sailed off across the green. Jonah's stomach knotted; this was going to be really bad or really funny, and he wasn't sure which.

Grace took her turn, and he watched her form with deep appreciation, especially her posterior as she bent down to set her ball and swung with her hips. It was effortless, the way her body moved to drive the ball down the green, going farther than Travis.

"Good shot, honey," Rick said proudly, and then he turned to Jonah. "You're next. I'll shoot last."

"Right." Jonah nodded and stepped up to the tee. He put his ball down and glanced over at Grace, who was nodding encouragingly.

Stupid golf, he cursed inwardly.

He took a deep breath and visualized the ball as he swung and connected with it. It sailed up into the sky.

"Wow," Grace exclaimed. "Great shot!"

"Thanks." Jonah had no idea where his ball landed, but he'd figure that out later. At least he didn't make an ass of himself by missing.

"I'm impressed," Rick admitted. "Grace, your husband has a great long shot. He might be a keeper."

The idea of being a keeper struck a chord with Jonah. He'd never been thought of as someone to be kept, except by his parents, and even then they weren't the most affectionate and never really expressed that sentiment out loud.

Hearing Rick say it made him feel good and it shouldn't have, because it wasn't true and it wasn't going to last. But still a part of him liked it. He liked being included.

Jonah stood to the side so Rick could take his

turn, and Rick patted him on the shoulder, giving him an "Atta boy."

Grace sidled up next to him. "You're smirking," she said under her breath.

"Well, I'm a keeper." He winked.

"Well, I think so," Grace stated, but then her eyes widened and a pink blush stained her cheeks. It thrilled him.

He raised his eyebrows in surprise. "You do?"

A sweet smile pressed across her lips. "I do."

Her admitting that made his heart beat a bit faster.

It means nothing. It's platonic. Don't get carried away.

He shook those emotions away as Rick took his shot.

"Good shot, Rick," Travis called out.

Grace stood on her tiptoes and made a kissy noise, to make fun of Travis slightly. *Suck-up.*

"Behave," Jonah warned teasingly.

Although he liked this side of her. Devious. A little competitive streak, but also light-hearted.

It had been a long hard day at work. They were both tired; that might've been why Grace was a bit giggly. Golf had been the last thing he wanted to do after his shift tonight, but with Grace here instead of her ex, maybe he would get through the evening after all. At least he was spending time with her. There might've been a time limit to their arrangement, but he was going to enjoy it fully.

* * *

They finished the game, and he didn't do too badly. He might have come in dead last, but it was so much fun spending the evening with Grace and joking around with her. After they'd finished, they went to the clubhouse to have dinner. The big boys' night out would be saved for later when Victor could come. That was fine by Jonah.

Even if it hadn't gone terribly, he'd still been stressed all day. When they got back to the condo, he was going to change and go for a swim. He needed that.

"That was a great evening." Grace sighed as they left the clubhouse. "I thought it was going to be so much worse."

"It was a good game. Thanks for the lesson. I think it helped."

"You did good," she agreed. "My dad seemed to like you. He was way more talkative tonight."

"I like him too. And your mom. If you don't mind me saying so, you really seem to want to please them."

Grace paused. "Do I?" she asked, startled.

"Well, I mean, this lie for starters—we're pretending to be married to keep them all happy. This whole farce is about that, pleasing them."

"I guess you're right."

"I didn't mean to upset you," he apologized. "I just honestly I don't think you have to try so hard."

"You didn't upset me. I guess it all stems back to my almost drowning."

"So you almost drown as a child, and now you have to make up for it?"

"Partly. I was in and out of hospitals right after. I was in a coma on life support for a while. There were a lot of expenses, things were sacrificed for me."

"That's not your responsibility," Jonah said gently.

"Isn't it? I disobeyed my parents and snuck into the pool."

He didn't know how to respond to that. He knew he was broaching a touchy subject with her and had to tread lightly. He didn't want to make her mad or push her away. "I think they love you and you worry too much."

She nodded. "Well, I guess it's my turn to ask you a hard question."

"Go for it."

"You swim every night, even when it's cold out. Why?"

"It's a coping tool to ease my anxiety. It helps. My therapist suggested it."

"Really?"

"Why so surprised?"

"You just seem so sure about yourself."

"It's been a lot of hard work." He cocked his head to the side. "Is that really what you wanted to ask me?"

Her shoulders slumped. "No. There's something else."

"As I said before, go for it. Ask away." Although he had a feeling he might regret this.

"Why did you agree to this charade?"

He turned to look her straight in the eye. Her arms were crossed, her mouth set in a firm line. It was a fair question and one that he'd been asking himself since he said he would do this for her.

"You never let a partner down. That much I've learned. Especially in my time with the Marines. I didn't want to let you down. I wanted to be there for you."

Her hard expression softened, and she looked away. "Well, thanks again for going along with it."

"Especially the golf bit. That was torture."

Her laugh rang out across the parking lot, and he liked making her laugh. All that tension and hard stuff melted away. "Well, yes, I suppose I owe you one for the golf."

"So you taught me to golf…how about I teach you to swim?" Jonah knew it was a long shot, but he wanted to help her get over her fear, to work on her PTSD when it came to drownings and water—and he wanted to change the subject. Although logically, he knew it would take more than just swimming lessons. She needed to talk it through with someone, just like he had. But at least he could offer this and help her.

Grace froze. "What?"

"Swimming. I can teach you."

She laughed nervously as they piled their gear into her trunk. "Victor tried to teach me once. He dunked me, if you remember. I don't go in pools."

"I do remember you telling me that. I swear, no dunking. I want to show you some moves so you can feel safe. It'll help ease your anxiety on the job when we're called in for those situations."

"I don't…"

"Trust me." It was a big ask.

He could see it all there. The trauma of what had happened to her was holding her back, and he wanted to help her. She was so strong and amazing. She could conquer this. He reached out and gently stroked her face, getting lost in her big brown eyes, her pulse was racing under his fingertips.

All he wanted to do was kiss her in that moment, but he resisted. Again. He seemed to be doing a lot of that around her lately.

It was monumental, him asking her to put her precarious faith in him, especially about something she was so terrified to do. But once upon a time she'd been more adventurous.

That was before Victor. And she was learning that she didn't have to diminish herself when she was around Jonah. Maybe, just maybe she could do this thing. Maybe she could go back to being that person she had been before.

She was still a bit shocked at the way this conversation was turning. They were tackling some deep stuff.

The way he had gotten her to open up to him was surprising, and the fact was she didn't mind it at all.

"Okay," she agreed quickly. "You can show me some stuff, but the moment you dunk me—well, it won't be a purple nurple that I'll inflict on your nipples. It'll be worse."

"How?"

"I'll tear them off."

"That sounds like a promise," he stuttered nervously, rubbing his chest.

"Oh. It is."

He winced. "Ouch. Noted."

They drove back to her place, took their gear inside and changed for swimming. All she had was a two-piece, from the rare times she'd sunbathe.

At first she hesitated because she thought it was too revealing for someone she worked with, for a friend, for Jonah. But the truth was he'd seen her naked, and vice versa.

And just thinking about that made her cheeks bloom with heat.

With need.

Stop that.

By the time she'd changed Jonah was already down at the pool. She was thankful it was empty so no one else had to see her completely scared of getting in the water. She opened the gate and made her way to the pool steps. Jonah paddled over and stood up. A few lustful notions about the water trailing down over his bronzed skin flittered in her mind.

It was like part of her was craving him, like he was the only cure for her affliction of lust. Her body definitely remembered their wedding night.

Mostly it remembered the pleasure.

"You ready?" he asked.

For what? she wanted to ask him, but she assumed he meant swimming and not what she had been thinking about.

"Nope." Her voice shook, like her body. Her knees were about ready to give out.

Jonah held out his hand. "I've got you."

Such simple words, and she wanted to believe them. She wanted to trust him, but it was hard.

He hasn't let you down yet. You can do this.

She reached out and took his hand, stepping slowly into the warn water. She remembered the freeing sensation of floating, how she'd loved it as a child, but then her throat clogged and it felt like she couldn't breathe as the panic overtook her. Her body was completely rigid, and she closed her eyes.

"It's okay." He slipped his arms around her. "I'll hold you. Tonight it's just about getting your footing. Ground yourself and feel the solid bottom beneath your heels. You're safe."

She nodded. "Okay."

"Come on." Jonah guided her through the water, and soon her body relaxed. His hand was on her waist, his fingers brushing her skin, his body warm and sturdy. Like a rock, something she could lean on. She'd never had that before.

"This is...this is okay."

"Does it feel good?" he asked.

"It does." She glanced up at him. Their gazes locked, and a rush of fire flowed through her veins. When she was with him, it felt so right. She was stronger and safe. Almost powerful again. Like she could do anything.

"You can let go of me," she said.

"You're sure?"

"Positive."

Jonah stepped away so she was on her own in waist-high water, and it was so thrilling. Scary but exhilarating as she stood there on her own feet, in a pool. Before her near drowning as a child, this was where she'd been so happy. Every summer she'd been in the water like a fish. She'd missed this.

She took a deep breath and on her own terms sank down below the surface, only for a second. Jonah's arms came around her as she stood up, sputtering and wiping the water from her eyes. A few nightmarish recollections flashed before her eyes—her mother's face, the feeling of fighting against the breathing tube—but they dissipated as she drank in the night air, telling her terrified body she was okay and that she could breathe.

"Amazing," he encouraged. "You did it."

"I don't think it worked. I'm still scared."

He smoothed back her hair gently. "This wasn't a quick fix."

"So how did you work on it all?"

"Cognitive behavioral therapy. Talking it out. Medication. There's nothing to be ashamed of."

"No. You're right." And looking at him she saw such a strong, caring man. One that made her weak in the knees.

She had to get out of here, out of his arms before she did something she regretted—or something she'd like very, very much.

"Thanks, but I think I'm done now."

Jonah didn't argue and guided her to the stairs. She clambered out of the pool and grabbed her towel, wrapping it tight around her like a security blanket.

"You okay?" he asked.

"Yeah. Cold. But yeah, I'm fine."

She was more than that. It felt like she'd conquered a mountain.

"Do you mind if I keep swimming? If you need me, I can come up with you."

"I'm good. Swim. I'm going to shower and head

to bed. I'm exhausted from work and golf, and tomorrow is that dinner with my family again."

"Right. I'll lock up. You did great, Grace. You should be proud."

And she was, but she was overcome with a lot of emotions in that moment, ones she couldn't quite put her finger on. Or maybe she didn't want to identify them, because she was scared what it all meant. Jonah had given her the courage she hadn't thought anyone could give her, because she'd always refused to let them. She'd only relied on herself.

"'Night."

She quickly headed back upstairs, turning once to watch him swim his laps. Jonah was so kind and caring. He completely helped her face her fear and believe in something she thought was impossible again.

And she couldn't help but wonder what else she'd been wrong about for all this time. Maybe she'd been wrong about marriage and love.

Grace didn't get much sleep that night. She tossed and turned, and when she did close her eyes all she could think about was Jonah and how he made her feel when she faced that huge fear of hers. How amazing he had been with her father, how her father had liked him and opened up. How kind and gentle he'd been with her in the pool. In that moment she had been safe with him. Even though she put on a brave face at work, that wasn't always a true reflection of the inside, and it had been a long time since she had felt that strong. It was a long time since she had truly believed in herself.

When she got up in the morning, Jonah wasn't there. He'd left a note that said he'd gone for a motorcycle ride but that he'd be back in the afternoon to go to her parents' place for dinner in St. George.

Instantly, she worried that maybe she had stepped over the line with him.

Maybe she was pushing him away. Victor used to get annoyed with her when she hid things. He'd blamed her for the failure of their relationship, and she'd shouldered that responsibility: She'd been too closed-off, he'd said. It had pushed him into the arms of his now wife.

Now she was trying to hide again, hide all the confusing feelings racing through her.

Feelings like hope.

Like love.

Stop going around in circles.

Maybe it wasn't her fault that he'd left this morning. Maybe none of this was her fault and she didn't have to shoulder this blame. They'd both agreed to this farce with her family. They were both in on this together. If Jonah needed some space, then that was fine with her.

Jonah will come back. It's your anxiety.

Disgusted with herself, she kept busy for the rest of the day. She ran errands, she took a walk, cleaned and then got ready for the trip to St. George. Jonah came back as promised. He cleaned up quickly. He didn't seem weird or aloof at all. He was totally at ease, which she slightly hated him for, because she wished she was a little bit more laid back like that right now.

When had he got so laidback?

She reminded herself it was just the mask he wore when he was around her family. It wasn't real. It was also proof that what she was feeling was one-sided and that she had to be careful with her heart. Someone who did care wouldn't be so at ease and would have spent a sleepless night brooding.

So yeah, they were completely one-sided, these emotions.

How could she be so foolish?

She didn't chat much during the car ride to St. George, but Jonah didn't seem to notice.

They made it to the family dinner. The conversation was easy and light. This time they were greeted like usual; there was no awkwardness at all. Her family seemed to have welcomed Jonah, and he got along so well with them. Even her dad was opening up. It warmed her to her core, but she dreaded to think what was going to happen when it all ended. Her mother had made Grace's favorite dinner of roast chicken and potatoes, but she had a hard time swallowing any of it. There was a time limit to this seemingly picture-perfect happiness. There was a court date in their future, and it was looming like a ticking time bomb.

"Grace swam yesterday," Jonah announced, starting a conversation and shaking Grace out of her racing thoughts.

Her mother's eyes widened. "What?"

Grace kicked Jonah under the table and then looked at her family's stunned faces. "It was nothing."

"But you don't swim," Aidan stammered. "Like...at all."

"Right. I don't," Grace corrected. "I went in the pool with Jonah."

"He's trying to teach you to swim again? That's great," Rick said. "I knew I liked you for a reason, Jonah."

Jonah beamed at her proudly. "She put her head under the water and everything."

"You did?" her mother asked, amazed. It almost looked like she was going to cry, and that was the last thing Grace wanted. Melanie's lips were a thin line, tightly pursed together, and instantly Grace felt bad for stealing the spotlight.

"It's no big deal. Can we talk about something else?" she asked, trying to change the subject.

"Sure," her father said. "So after Melanie's wedding in a couple of weeks, we're going to throw you and Jonah a wedding reception at the club."

She exchanged a concerned glance with Jonah, who was clearly trying to hide his shock.

"Dad, you don't have to do to the trouble," she said quickly, hoping it would dissuade him from the idea. That kind of event came with a price tag, and she didn't want her parents to spend it on something that wasn't real.

"Sure I do," Rick argued. "You're my daughter and it's right."

"I'm sad I didn't get to see much of Mr. and Mrs. Cute Paramedic's wedding," her mom teased.

"Yeah. It was blurry," Melanie giggled, a little unkindly. "We didn't even get to see the kiss over the altar. The one sealing the deal."

If Grace could reach out under the table and kick her little sister, she would. Jonah looked at her like he was ready to bolt out the front door, and she couldn't blame him.

"We kissed. I can't help that our video guy was also drunk that night," Grace replied through tight lips.

"Why don't you just kiss now?" Aidan suggested, shrugging. Grace shot her little brother a death glare.

"Yes. Kiss now." Melanie held up her wineglass and tapped it, like people did at weddings.

She was giving a saucy look, and Grace knew Melanie was just doing this to irritate her. She'd noogie Melanie later.

Grace glanced at Jonah, silently apologizing

to him. Now she wished they were still talking about her swimming.

"It's okay, sweetie," he said stiffly. "It's not like it's the first time."

Which was true—it wasn't. She didn't really recall the first time, but she had foggy memories of the few times after and how much she had liked them. Just thinking about kissing Jonah again made her nipples harden, her body clench in anticipation.

A jittery, butterfly sensation swirled in the pit of her stomach.

She didn't want to kiss him again because she had promised him they wouldn't. But she also did want it.

Badly.

I can do this.

She closed her eyes, her body trembling in a mixture of both dread and excitement, her emotions racing as she felt the light touch of the tip of his nose brushing against hers.

"It's okay. Breathe," he whispered, his breath hot against her neck. That simple reassurance eased her, and she leaned in as his lips brushed against hers in a feather-light kiss that made her burn for more.

The kiss deepened quickly as she sank into the pleasure of giving in to what she wanted.

Him.

Her body ached for him. His hand cupped her

cheek as his tongue slipped past her lips. It was like she was melting, and she wanted to stay in this moment longer.

Then someone cleared their throat and she remembered that they weren't alone. They were at a family dinner. She broke away from the kiss, her cheeks flaming with heat. Jonah didn't move, his eyes dark with need, which was what she was feeling keenly in this moment. It was a hunger, a longing they just couldn't indulge in.

"Wow," Melanie said. "That was some kiss. Almost like a first kiss."

"Well, every time I kiss her it's like the first time," Jonah murmured, his eyes locked on her, hooking her soul and making her insides melt.

"I thought it was gross," Aidan stated, breaking the sizzling tension in the air.

"You're the one who suggested it," Travis quipped.

"Yeah, but I assumed it'd be a peck or something. Bleh." Aidan shuddered.

Her mother laughed, and the conversation resumed, except Grace knew things had changed in that moment. Maybe not for Jonah, but definitely for her. And she had to figure out how she was going to protect herself from being shattered when this all ended.

CHAPTER EIGHT

To say that he slept well that night was a big fat lie. Jonah didn't actually mind the couch; the reason he didn't get a wink of sleep was the fact that he couldn't stop thinking about that kiss with Grace. The sensation was plaguing him, burning through him like a fever, and he wanted more.

They'd kissed before. That was obvious from that blurry video and all his fuzzy-edged memories, but he'd meant what he said to Melanie. That kiss in St George really had felt like the first one. It had been intoxicating.

If there hadn't been people around, he would have let it go on forever. When Grace's lips had parted and their tongues had entwined, every fiber in his being, every nerve ending had lit up like a Christmas tree.

Thankfully, someone had piped up and brought him back to reality. He had remembered she wasn't his.

It was all an act.

Even though he kept repeating that over and

over in his head, it didn't do him any good in the sleep department. Eventually, he gave up, had a shower and dragged himself to work.

Grace had left earlier to attend a meeting with the chief of the station house, which wasn't strange or unusual. Senior partners were called in once a month for a state-of-the-union kind of meeting. Jonah didn't mind losing his ride. He could use the walk in.

After grabbing coffee at a local coffee shop, he got to the station just as their patrol was about to start. And just as they had promised each other, there was no time for chatting or focusing on the awkwardness that was now between them. They'd sworn that this would not affect their work and he aimed to keep that promise. Work came first.

But it was hard not to think about how soft Grace's lips had been or how she had melted against him when they kissed. How he had drunk in the taste of her, the scent of her. He wanted more.

So much more.

He wanted to run his hands over her body, touch her skin, bring her to pleasure. He wanted to care for her, cherish her. It had been long time since he'd even contemplated a relationship. Since his married had ended, he had resigned himself to the fact it was just him. It was lonely but okay. He could keep his feelings in check.

Now he was starting to think he wanted more

with a woman who didn't want him. Or at the very least didn't want to be tied down.

As they finished up a call that hadn't required them to transport anyone, he could tell that she was watching him and that she wanted to say something.

"I know you're staring at me," he said offhandedly.

"Sorry. It's...about last night."

"No." He turned around quickly. "When I agreed to this whole thing the promise was that it wouldn't get weird."

"But it did. Right?"

He relaxed, not realizing how tense he was holding his body. "Yeah, I suppose it did."

"I still want to have you as my partner. I don't want that to change." She swallowed hard. "When I checked my email this morning, I got something from the courthouse. We've been given a date to end the marriage."

The moment that she uttered those words, his stomach sank to the soles of his feet. Logically, he'd known it was coming, but maybe he just wasn't as prepared for it as he thought he might be.

"Oh, when is it?" he asked, trying to be nonchalant about it.

"Three days after my sister's wedding. How is that for timing?" she joked dryly.

"Terrible."

She nodded. "Well, at least the not knowing isn't hanging over our heads any longer."

"No," he exhaled. Then he bit his tongue for a moment, because there was a part of him that wanted to blurt out that he wanted to be with her.

That kiss they'd shared had stirred up everything he'd been trying to hold back. His desire for Grace, his need for her... It burned deep within him.

For the first time in a long time, he wanted to explore something more with someone. With Grace.

Something physical.

Friends with benefits?

A preposterous thought. Even suggesting it was risky. She might not want him, and he really didn't want to face rejection. Especially not from her.

Not from Grace.

It would ruin their friendship and definitely sour their working relationship. Or...would it?

When Mona had turned against him, when he'd come home, when she hadn't wanted to help him get through the grief of Justin's death and then cheated on him, *that* had been a rejection. Thinking about Grace doing the same didn't make any sense.

She was so different from his ex. She was more like his best friend.

Like Justin.

Still, it was hard to find the words or take the chance.

She won't reject you.

Jonah ignored that little niggle itching at the back of his mind. Even after all this time it was so hard to believe that if he put himself out there that he wouldn't be setting himself up for heartbreak.

Dispatch called, snapping him out of his reverie.

"Rig three, requested presence at an accident scene. Pedestrian struck. Peakness Pass and South Grand Canyon Road South."

Grace hit the button on the radio on her sleeve. "Ten-four and copy that. En route."

There was no more talking now as they had work to do. They got everything loaded back up, and Grace climbed into the driver's seat as Jonah took down the information scrolling on the computer screen about the accident. The sirens came on, and Grace drove through the streets of Vegas until they got to the Summerlin intersection, which was a residential area and not a main thoroughfare. Still, people were known to speed through these side streets.

The police were already present. He could see the flashing lights. A car was pulled over, and the police were questioning the driver.

"At least it wasn't a hit-and-run," Grace remarked.

"That's something." Jonah scanned through the

milling people, and his heart sank when he saw it was a child who was lying on the ground. "Crap."

Grace frowned. "Yeah."

She pulled the ambulance over, and they moved quickly to get their equipment out of the back. Grace went over to talk to the police officer who was waving them down. No doubt he had pertinent information for them.

Jonah made his way to the little boy, who looked broken and was being cradled by his mother. The boy's mother was calling his name over and over as she rocked slightly. What struck Jonah, like a thunderbolt from the sky, was how much the little boy looked like Justin had when they were kids. There were so many similarities—the hair color, the facial features. The sight of the blood draining from that face made Jonah sick to his stomach.

Then an image flashed through his mind. Justin, in his arms, the life light draining from his eyes as Jonah begged him to hold on.

His breathing quickened, the world spinning.

You need to focus.

Swallowing hard, he locked it all away. Just like his therapist had taught him: compartmentalize and focus on the task at hand.

"Ma'am, my name is Jonah, and I'm a paramedic. Can you tell me what happened while I take a look at your son?"

"Sure," the woman responded with a wobbly

voice. "Justin and I were walking, and then we heard this screech and I looked behind to see that car over there jump the curb. Justin went flying."

Justin. Even the name triggered him, but Jonah tried to ignore the flood of emotions, the trauma from when he'd held Justin for the last time.

"Was he conscious when he hit the ground?" he asked, checking Justin's pupils. One had blown, but the other was still reacting. There was no doubt in his mind that there was a brain bleed and broken bones. It wouldn't be surprising given the impact and how small and young the boy was.

"He was," Justin's mother sobbed.

"Justin, can you hear me?" Jonah asked, checking for the sound of breathing and assessing whether the air way was clear.

Grace knelt down on the other side. "The police filled me in on what was happening."

"I'm worried about spinal damage from the force of the impact. We need to get him on a backboard," Jonah stated.

Grace nodded, and they set to work stabilizing Justin so they could load him up and take him to the children's emergency room at the nearby hospital. They used braces to stabilize the neck and strapped him down. He was easier to lift as he was just a small child. If Jonah had to guess the boy might've been around seven. Way too young to have such a bad accident.

"We're going to take Justin to the children's

hospital," Grace explained to Justin's mother. "You can come with us. We're going to get fluids and oxygen into him."

Justin's mother nodded. "Okay. What about the police?"

"They'll know where to find you," Jonah answered. "We have to get your boy healthy again."

Justin's mother nodded and followed them as they lifted Justin onto their gurney and got him in the back of the ambulance. Grace knew all the streets like the back of her hand, and Jonah wanted to stay with the boy, so he stayed put, taking care of his little patient.

Grace locked up, and Jonah worked on the IV and monitors. There was no way, if he could help it, that he was going to let this Justin die. Not on his watch.

Come on, buddy, he silently entreated.

There was a pulse, but it was rapid and thready. Justin's blood pressure was high. Jonah drowned out the sounds of the siren as Grace called into the emergency department at the local children's hospital.

"Talk to me, Crandall," Grace said over her shoulder as she drove. "Need some stats for the dispatch desk."

"BP is elevated. Using permissive hypotension en route to stabilize. Suspect fractures and blunt force trauma, possible subdural hematoma."

Grace nodded and repeated everything back

the hospital emergency room dispatch. They turned the corner and headed straight into the ambulance bay. The moment they pulled up a team of trauma surgeons in gowns rushed out to meet them. Grace parked and jumped out of the rig to open the door, rattling off information to the doctors.

"Patient is a male, aged seven. Blunt force trauma after being struck by a motor vehicle. Thrown approximately two hundred yards. Was conscious after the crash, but was unconscious upon our arrival to the scene. Trituration of permission hypotension used in field. Bolus of fluid, central line started."

"Left pupil nonresponsive," Jonah stated as he helped lift the gurney down. "Right pupil normal. Breath sounds shallow."

Grace had a doctor sign the release forms, and Jonah walked in with the gurney into the trauma bay. He helped the doctors as they transferred Justin onto a hospital stretcher.

"Thank you," a doctor said. "We've got it from here."

It was Jonah's cue to leave, but he had a hard time pulling away. Logically, he knew the boy wasn't his Justin, but he still didn't want to leave him. He wanted to stay, to make sure the boy was going to make it.

Watching the doctors work over Justin, the little boy, it felt like Jonah was a million miles away, and he closed his eyes, trying to steady himself enough to move.

"Jonah?" Grace asked, coming up beside him. She laid a hand on his shoulder. "Come on."

He nodded and let Grace lead him out of the trauma bay. There was nothing more he could. He'd done his job, so why did he still feel like he failed?

Not much was said the rest of their shift, because Jonah was still struggling with how to process it all. Constant thoughts of his best friend ran through his mind. He was quiet at dinner, and Grace didn't pry, which he appreciated. After dinner he went for his usual swim, but it was like a switch had been flicked on in his brain. One that held back his emotions about Justin, his failed marriage, Grace. And try as he might, using all his usual techniques and tactics, today he couldn't compartmentalize it all and lock it away again.

Visions of the accident kept morphing into the whole scene of Justin's death, playing over and over again behind his eyes like a bad, tormenting horror show that he couldn't escape from, and he tried to fight back, to right the wrongs, but he couldn't manage it. He couldn't save him. It was always out of his grasp, and he tried to fight back the screams.

"Jonah," Grace whispered.

He jolted away. Her hands were on him; it was

dark, and he was in the living room. He hadn't thought he'd fallen asleep. It was like a waking dream.

"What time is it?" he asked, groggily.

"Two in the morning," she replied. "Are you okay?"

"It was a nightmare. Nothing to worry about." He tried to roll over on the narrow couch. He didn't want Grace to fuss. Mona would get so annoyed when he'd have these lapses.

Grace. Isn't. Mona.

Still, she didn't need to see this side of him.

"You were screaming," she said, gently rubbing his back. "I don't think it was nothing."

Her touch was soothing, and he couldn't remember the last time he'd been comforted so sweetly. He should've just pushed her away, but he couldn't. He needed her here with him. He rolled over. "I was having flashbacks. Thinking of my best friend who died in my arms overseas, how I couldn't save him. It's a symptom of my PTSD."

"Justin, right?"

He nodded. "I'm sorry for waking you up. I'll be okay."

Grace stood up, and then she took his hand. "Come."

"Where?"

"You're coming to bed with me. We can share a bed. I don't think you should be alone tonight."

Jonah had no fight left in him at that point, and

she was right about one thing—he didn't want to be alone. He grabbed his pillow and followed Grace into her bedroom.

"One thing though," she said with a serious tone, spinning around.

"What's that?"

"You sleep with your head on the pillows this time. No feet up there."

He laughed, softly hoping his voice didn't shake. "Deal."

She pulled back the covers, and he got settled. The sheets smelled liked her, which was no surprise. He loved that soft, sweet smell of her. It was vanilla and something else. It should have been soothing; instead, all he could think about was her lying next to him. And he didn't want to close his eyes and have this end or have a repeat of the nightmare he'd been having.

"That case rattled you today," she said. "It's because his name was Justin, wasn't it?"

"It was."

"I called the hospital after you fell asleep."

"Oh?" he asked, his interest piqued.

"He's going to make it. He came through surgery just fine. What you did to control his blood pressure helped save him."

Relief washed through him. "He looked a lot like Justin did when we were kids and had the same name. It was all…"

"I understand. Trust me. I still remember the

moment I almost drowned. I remember when I woke up fighting the tube. Water triggers me, so I understand those dreams."

"My ex didn't."

Grace grunted. "I'm not her. You said to me that I was safe with you. Well, you're safe with me."

That meant everything to him.

He leaned on his elbow to stare down at her in the darkness, her blond hair loose over her pillow. There was a thin beam of light sneaking through her blinds from the streetlights outside. It made her skin glow, and he could see her eyes sparkling. He touched her face, gently, brushing the tips of his fingers over her silken skin, reveling in the softness. He wanted to stay here forever, in this moment.

"Grace," he whispered huskily. "I think I'm going to have to sleep on the couch."

"Why?" her voice hitched in her throat.

He wanted to stay, but there was no way he could. "Because I'm scared. I want you more than I can bear it."

She let out a gasp, just a quick one, as she processed what he said to her, because she'd thought it was all one sided, those raw emotions she'd been grappling with. It appeared, by his own admission, that Jonah was feeling the same.

She couldn't promise him forever, but she could

give him tonight. Because she wanted that now more than anything.

She wanted him close to her, nothing between them. The mattress dipped as he got up to leave, and she reached out, grabbing his arm to stop him.

"Stay. Be with me." Her voice shook as she said it out loud.

"And what about beyond tonight?" he asked. "I don't know what the future holds."

"I don't need forever. Just tonight."

"I don't have protection."

"I think we're okay. We didn't have it on our wedding night, and I'm on the pill. Stay. I want this, Jonah. I want you."

And it was exactly what she wanted. She wanted to be selfish in this moment with him. She was done fighting all these feelings.

He hesitated, only for a moment, and then gathered her up into his arms. "I want you too, Grace. I've been burning for you for a long time."

Jonah kissed her again with an intensity that she felt keenly deep within her soul. All she wanted to do was touch and taste every inch of him.

Part of her wanted to savor this moment, but the other part of her, the one that had been not so patiently waiting, wanted this to be as fast and furious as the insatiable need that was burning a hole deep within her.

Being with him right now was a huge gamble because she didn't want to leave anything to chance with them. She didn't want the awkwardness if things went south; she didn't want it to affect their partnership or their friendship. She didn't want Jonah to feel like he had to stay away from her. But as he kissed her, his hands burning her skin with his fiery touch, she was willing to bet away every last inch of herself to be with him in this moment.

Her body thrummed with electric need as they made quick work of their clothes so that there was nothing between them. It was just the two of them now, naked and vulnerable to each other. Jonah ran his hands over her body, trailing over her curves slowly, making her hunger for him.

"You make me so hard, Grace."

Grace kissed him again, pulling him closer as she touched him. He leaned over her, cupping her breasts, running his thumb over her pink nipple.

"Tell me what you want," she mewled.

"I want to bury myself inside you." He stroked her between her legs, making her wet with need as she gripped his shaft, touching the hard velvety skin.

Jonah moaned and jerked against her palm as she stroked him.

"Do you like that?" she teased.

"You're killing me, Grace."

"I want you, Jonah." She wanted to tell him that

she only wanted him, but she couldn't formulate the right words. She arched her back, pleasure coursing through her as his tongue circled her sensitive nipple.

She raised her hips, silently begging him to take her, possess her.

Then he was at her entrance, hot and hard as he slowly slid inside, filling every inch of her, and she succumbed to the heady sensations of letting go to Jonah, of being vulnerable to him.

His thrusts came quicker, more urgent, and she met the rhythm of his pace, clinging to every heightened sensation. Her fingers dug into his shoulders. She came hard and fast, crying out as she tightened around him.

In this moment she wanted this to last for an eternity, but she knew it couldn't. She didn't want to think about the eventual end or else she'd cry.

Jonah's thrusts became shallow, quicker, and his hands held on to her hips tight as he rode her. He cried out as he finished and rolled over onto his back, pulling her tight against his chest where she could listen to his heart racing under her ear. It was soothing.

He wrapped his arms around her, holding her, like he too knew their time together was fleeting. He ran his fingers down her back. "What're you thinking about?"

"About us. This."

"I know. Me too. I promise it won't affect our work."

"I know it won't." She laughed softly. "What about friends with benefits? Or partners with benefits."

He grunted. "Wife-and-husband with benefits you mean."

"Something like that," she chided.

"Oh, I think I can make that work." And he kissed her again, down her neck and over her stomach.

She giggled as his lips trailed lower. She wasn't going to think any more about the end, the court date, the fake marriage. Tonight all she wanted was him. Everything else could wait.

CHAPTER NINE

It was nice to wake up holding her the next day. It took Jonah a moment to realize that he was not on the couch and that he was in Grace's bed. Then it all came back to him in stunning clarity, and when he cracked open his eye, he saw her there, in his arms sleeping peacefully.

No wonder he'd had a dreamless sleep.

A comfortable sleep.

Actually, he couldn't remember the last time he had slept so soundly. It had been badly needed. He shifted slightly to get up, trying not to stir her, but she opened her eyes and then smiled at him.

"Good morning," she said, her voice a bit muffled.

"Did I wake you?" he asked.

"No." She rolled onto her side, tucking her hands under her head. "We might've slept in."

He glanced at the alarm clock. "It's seven. We didn't sleep in that much, and our shift starts in, like, an hour and half."

"Yours does."

He cocked an eyebrow. "What do you mean?"

"I have to go for training at Vegas Central. Something about new protocols. All shift leaders are going at separate times. So you'll be with John today."

"Well, I'm a bit disappointed."

"Because you'll miss me?"

"Yes, but also John is boring," he groaned.

Grace laughed gently. "So? He thinks you are too. He likes to chat, and you don't."

Jonah moaned. "I'm a loner, remember?"

"Were, I believe."

"Still, disappointed."

"Same. I really don't want to spend the day with Victor. I'd rather spend it with you."

"About work…" He trailed off because he really didn't want to ruin this lovely morning by talking about what happened, but then he didn't want it to affect their work either.

"I know. We've been doing well so far. I don't think this will be a problem."

"You sound so certain," he mused.

"Of course. We're adults, and there's an end date."

Jonah sensed a bit of sadness in her voice when she mentioned the looming court date. It was bothering him too. Last night had been so wonderful, so magical. It was everything that he had wanted for the last couple of weeks. Actually, if he was honest with himself, he'd been attracted to her the first time he met her. It had just been easier to ignore that attraction when they were nothing more than partners and he didn't know anything about her.

Now he was getting to know her. She wasn't just this woman he worked with. She was turning into so much more. Even more than a friend, and it was a bit paralyzing to even think about trying to take it further. Grace had said she wasn't like his ex-wife and that was true, but it was still hard to trust himself to her, especially when it came to his heart.

He also didn't want to hurt her either. Grace had been through so much too.

He should've felt bad about making love to her last night. He didn't regret it at all. In that moment, being vulnerable with her was exactly what he wanted.

What he needed.

"You've gone quiet again. You okay?" she asked.

"I'm fine. I think everything will be all right. Though I don't know how, given I have to listen to John's boring stories at the station all day."

Grace laughed and then kissed him on his lips. "Remember—we said friends with benefits. We can make this work."

"Are you saying you wouldn't mind a repeat of last night?" He asked, intrigued.

"Maybe." She grinned. He reached for her, and

she ducked away. "Later. How about a motorcycle ride out to the Red Rock Canyon after work? We can find a place to eat."

"You want to go for a motorcycle ride?" he questioned.

"I do." She stood up, and he admired her nakedness, groaning inwardly that she was being all responsible and getting ready for work. "Don't look at me like that."

"Like what?"

She frowned, only slightly. "I have to get ready for work, and so do you."

"Right, boss."

She nodded. "Get ready. And tonight we'll have a nice evening out and talk."

"Sounds good."

And it did. He wouldn't mind getting on his motorcycle tonight with her on the back. The last time she'd been on his bike his nipple had come away a bit bruised, but it would the worth it to share the evening with her. If she wrapped her legs around his waist, he didn't care if she ripped his nipples right off.

She was also very astute. They needed to talk about it all. They needed to talk about what happened last night, their friendship and the court date.

They needed an exit strategy, but as he watched her walk to the shower, he was wishing that they didn't need to have this talk.

For the first time in a long time, he didn't want an exit strategy. It scared him a little, but he pushed the fear away. He was pretty sure this strange sense of comfort was a blip, a fleeting thing and completely based on endorphins.

It couldn't be anything else, could it?

The day without Grace was long and just as boring as Jonah had predicted. John was a nice enough guy. They just didn't have a lot in common. He prattled on and on about things, half of which Jonah couldn't even keep up with, and he had labeled himself a player. That was definitely not Jonah's ideal.

Remaining single was one thing, but maintaining bachelorhood to sleep around was another, and that was not what he wanted at all.

At least they weren't stuck in a rig together. Today was the day that John and Jonah remained at the station house, sort of on call and dealing with dispatch. Jonah usually preferred to be out in an ambulance, but without Grace it wasn't the same, so he was more than okay to putter around at the station.

Grace came back to the station house after a long day and looked absolutely exhausted. Once their shift was over, they headed back to their condo and got changed for a bike ride through the desert.

She had put on her denim jeans, a ripped

T-shirt and Docker boots. She looked like she was ready to kick some ass at all-night rave.

"Is this okay?" she asked, spinning around so he could look at her.

He grinned slowly. "Just missing a leather jacket."

"Well, I don't have one of those."

"Honestly, I wouldn't mind seeing you in a bit more leather, if I'm honest."

She quirked an eyebrow. "Oh? Do tell."

"That'll wait. Come on—before we lose the light." He handed her the pink helmet he'd bought her, and they went down to his bike.

She climbed on behind him, her arms going around his torso. The heat from her body, her breasts pressed against the back of him, just made him hunger for more and an image of parking somewhere off the highway and bending her over the seat of the motorcycle flashed through his mind and made him hard with need.

Something that wouldn't make this bike ride any easier.

Well, you did promise her a ride...you just didn't specify.

They drove off to the Red Rock Canyon, northwest of Las Vegas. It was a gorgeous night. There were no winds rushing down off the mountain, the heat of the day was dissipating, and as they approached the canyon the red seemed to be even more vibrant, like just after a rain. They drove around the canyon area on the highway.

Although they couldn't talk, Grace was completely relaxed. Her grip on him wasn't as tight as before, and it was almost natural to have her on the back of his bike. He could do this forever.

Just north of the red rocks there was a little diner. It wasn't the fifties diner that was on the highway to California—that was in the opposite direction—but it looked like a fun little place and there were other bikes parked outside, in a mix of family cars.

The music was loud, and there was a lot of neon.

It looked like it would have fit in on the old Route 66. *Kitschy* was the word. It was the perfect place to have a nice dinner and talk.

He was somewhat dreading the conversation, but they needed to discuss what had happened between them last night and where they went from here.

In a couple of weeks Grace's sister was getting married, and then a couple days after that, they had their court date and their marriage would be over. They had to come up with a contingency plan for the eventual demise.

There were too many people involved now, and he really didn't want to see her family get hurt.

The waitress at the diner took them to a corner booth, and they slipped in across the vinyl seats.

The retro music was loud, but it wasn't overpowering, and their little corner booth had a window that overlooked the desert and the setting sun.

The waitress left them with two menus and said she would be back in a bit.

"How did you find this place?" Grace asked.

"Just now."

"You didn't know about it before?"

"No."

"You drove to it."

He chuckled. "That's the fun of just going for a drive. Especially on a bike."

"I can see the appeal." She glanced down at her menu.

"So how was the workshop today?"

Grace groaned. "Tedious. Victor was acting all weird. He was super nice to me. He just usually blows me off. I think Travis had been telling him how well you got along with my father."

Jonah grinned. "Well, he's my father-in-law. I want to make a good impression."

"Well, Victor was always a bit possessive. My dad liked him, but I suspect he likes you more."

His heart sank. "For now."

She sighed sadly. "Right."

"I'm nervous about all of this. What're we going to do?"

"I guess we take it one day at a time."

He nodded. "No promises."

Grace worried her bottom lip. "Right. That's what we agreed."

The waitress came back with waters and then took their order before disappearing again. "Why doesn't your family know about what Victor did to you?"

He was hoping this time she'd tell him the truth, open up to him, that she'd be vulnerable with him. Always, Grace was trying to be so strong. Maybe he wasn't the only one perpetuating a facade. It worried him.

The question stung, like a slap to the face, but she couldn't blame Jonah for asking her again, because she really didn't know the answer herself. Now she could see all the red flags when it came to Victor. How come she hadn't seen that before? Why had she been so swept away by him in the past? The only thing she could think of was that she was a people pleaser.

She had fallen in love with the idea of having the most perfect relationship, one that would make her family happy and make them proud of her. Victor had been too good to be true, and she saw that now. She hadn't really been happy for a long time, because she'd been striving so hard to please everyone else around her.

She was never out to please herself.

The only thing that made her truly happy in life was her work.

And Jonah, a little voice piped up.

He made her happy in a way that she hadn't known was possible.

In a way she wasn't sure that she truly deserved it, but she wanted to hold on to it, she just wasn't sure how.

"I guess because I didn't want to seem like a failure to them again. And it's silly now in retrospect, because when this ends, when they learn the truth about us, it's going to let them down. It's going to disappoint them."

Jonah nodded. "I get that. I clung to my ex-wife because I foolishly thought that we had a strong bond, but when I married her, it was for all the wrong reasons. Fresh out of school, she was the high school sweetheart and I seemed like the life of the party."

"You mean you're not?" she chided.

"Not the way she wanted."

"And what about you?"

"I didn't want that life. Being the popular guy was lonely. I know now it was all an act."

"You're social with me," she said. "Well, now, but not at first."

"I trust you. You bring it out of me."

The idea that he trusted her made her flush with happiness. It was so flattering to have that effect on him, to know that he cared for her.

You don't know that for sure.

She nodded slowly, trying to push away those

doubts. "What you said before was right—we just have to take this day by day. And we already know that we're going to stay friends and that we can work together."

"And the lie?"

Grace took a deep breath. "I'm going to tell my family before the court date."

"We both will." Then he reached out and took her hand, giving it a squeeze to comfort her. It was reassuring. It was like they were in this together, more than just work partners.

"So tell me all about your day with John."

Jonah groaned and rolled his eyes. "It was the usual. If you know John."

"Oh, I know John."

"What, did you have a secret marriage with him too?" he teased.

Grace kicked him playfully under the table. "Cracks like that, Mr. Cute Paramedic, are going to get you relegated back to the couch."

Jonah cocked an eyebrow. "Oh, you're letting me share your bed again tonight?"

There was a husky promise in the way he asked that question. It made her insides turn to jelly and her body tremble in anticipation.

"You said friends with benefits. And why else would I agree so easily to a bike ride tonight?"

There was a devious but hungry glint to his eye as he smiled. "I kind of like this bad-girl, rebellious side to you. I mean, I was seriously attracted to the scotch-drinking badass that I knew every day, but I like this side too."

"Well, we're living a lie as husband and wife. We might as well have a little fun with it, right?"

"Oh, yes. Do you think it would be okay if I canceled our food and asked for the check now?"

Grace laughed. "I'm hungry. Eat first, and then we'll take the bike back home."

He nodded. "Sounds like a plan."

She was relieved that he was on the same page as her, that this wasn't going to be as complicated as her anxiety had been telling her. Maybe, just maybe it would be easy with Jonah.

And there was a small glimmer of hope that maybe they might not need that court date after all. She wasn't going to fully invest in the dream just yet, but as they both agreed, they were going to just take this one day at a time and see where it led them.

She knew where it was going to lead them tonight after dinner, and that was enough to get by on now. Like she had said to him before, she didn't need promises of forever right now. She just needed to live in this moment.

She just needed tonight.

CHAPTER TEN

Two weeks later

IT HAD BEEN a magical two weeks since they'd first spent the night together and talked about their expectations going forward. There was still no promise of forever. Everything was as it was supposed to be, and their arrangement wasn't affecting their work.

The court date that would mark the end of their marriage was still in the back of her mind, but that was where she was keeping it. She didn't want to dwell on it.

Right now, she was doing something she hadn't done in a long time, and that was enjoying herself and not worrying about expectations from others. There was no need to people-please with Jonah, which was a relief. They had decided to take it one day at a time and that's exactly what she was doing. Every day was a new opportunity.

It was easy and fun.

She never thought she'd like a friends-with-benefits arrangement, but she was kind of enjoying it. In the rig, they just continued to work seamlessly together and there was no awkwardness or unprofessional behavior. There was just lots of teasing when they weren't treating patients.

And any kind of little tease played out later in the privacy of their home.

It still rattled her a bit to think of her condo as *their* home. She only ever really thought of it as a place to come and sleep, eat, rest after work. She'd never conceptualized it as a home until Jonah moved in.

Then she began to look forward to her time off. To days off on the couch and movies, to dinner and chores. To laughter.

And the idea it would eventually end made her sad.

Maybe it doesn't have to end?

But she ignored that little spark of hope. She wouldn't let it in.

She couldn't.

Everything was going smoothly, and she wanted to keep it that way. There was a part of her that was holding her breath until the other shoe dropped. When it came time for her sister's wedding and they were packing up her car to go to St. George, she couldn't help but wonder when disaster would strike.

"Do you think they'll separate us?" Jonah teased as they pulled their suitcases out.

"How do you mean?" she asked, distracted by her thoughts.

"Separate bedrooms."

"Why would they do that? We're married."

"Oh, good. I've kind of gotten used to sleeping next to you."

Grace flushed. "Same. I think I'm used to your snoring."

He rolled his eyes. "I don't think we'll be able to do our usual bedtime routine."

"Our..." She trailed off as she thought about it. "Right, no, probably not. If they put us where I think they will, it'll be my old childhood bedroom, and yeah, that's right next to my parents' room."

"Well, you could be a rebel and make out in your room." He waggled his eyebrows, and she smacked him playfully.

"You need to behave."

"Yes, boss."

She liked this more open version of Jonah. He was still a bit of an introvert, but with her things were easy and all awkwardness was gone. As they walked up to her parents' house, his back stiffened, and she knew he was struggling with the idea of all the extra people. If she could leave with him right now, she would.

She opened the door, and her mother was rushing around in a tizzy. Melanie looked a bit on edge too. Aidan walked by and rolled his eyes;

he was headed to the basement to get away from the chaos, no doubt. It was taking all Grace's willpower not to turn around, go home and just drive in for the wedding the next day. Or at the very least find a hotel so she and Jonah could relax.

"Hi, Mom. Sorry we're late, but..." Grace started to say.

"It's good you're here. You can take your bags to your room and then come back down." Her mother rushed off again.

Jonah was smirking. "She's a pretty good drill sergeant."

It was a cute joke, but she could see his trepidation under the surface. He was like her, a bit of a sponge who sucked in emotions of others around them. It was easy to shut it off at work, so why was it so hard here?

Because you care about your family.

And her heart skipped a beat, wondering if Jonah cared about *her*. He was so good at keeping his guard up, pretending around her family, but here now she saw a glimmer of him.

The real him.

Was that why it was hard for him to keep his guard up? Because he cared for her?

"Yes. It seems so. Come on and follow me."

They carried their bags upstairs and then down to almost the end of the hall. Her bedroom door still had her old childhood name plate on the white-paneled door.

"Will you still have posters up of your teenage crushes?"

Grace rolled her eyes. "No."

"No boy bands?"

Now that they were away from the chaos downstairs he was relaxing more, because it was just the two of them. This was the Jonah she knew intimately.

The Jonah she was starting to fall for.

A knot tightened in her stomach, and she took a step away from him. The realization scared her. She couldn't fall for a man when there was a quantifiable end date in sight.

"What is with you tonight?" Grace asked as she opened the door to her bedroom and flicked on the light.

Jonah was visibly disappointed as he walked in. "Rats. I was hoping to see some version of your past self in here."

"Oh? And what was your room like as a kid, old man?"

"Basic. Sports and that kind of stuff. I listened to a lot of heavy metal."

Grace quirked an eyebrow. "What?"

"Why is that surprising to you?"

"I don't know. You just don't—Wait a minute, I take that back. You ride a motorcycle and you wear leather. You're right. I shouldn't be shocked."

Jonah laughed. "I like metal music. I like banging my head, yes. But I never had my hair long."

She snickered. "I'm trying to picture you with long hair, and I can't. Every time I get a vision of you with long hair I see you with a flowing shirt on the cover one of those old romance novels, hair blowing in the breeze on a pirate ship."

"Is that a fantasy of yours?" he asked in a sultry tone.

"No."

He took a step closer and put his arms around her, pulling her body tight against him. Just that simple act made her ache with need. She liked the sensation of his hard body pressed against hers. He leaned down and kissed her slowly, teasing her.

"Are you sure?"

"No," she replied breathlessly.

He grinned that wicked grin that drove her wild. She forgot all about being at her parents' place and the fact that her family was waiting on her...until her mother rapped on the door and opened it.

"Grace!"

Grace and Jonah broke apart like they'd been caught doing something they shouldn't and were being scolded.

"What, Mom? Jeez," Grace said.

"I asked you to drop your bags and come downstairs. I need you both. This's no time for canoodling."

Grace groaned. "*Canoodling*, Mom? Seriously?"

Her mother frowned. "It's *all hands on deck* for

this wedding. Get downstairs. Oh, Jonah, would you be a love and drive Aunt Gert back to her house? It's getting late, and Gert doesn't do well in the dark."

Jonah nodded. "Sure thing, Leslie. I wonder if something is obscuring her vision."

Grace stifled her chuckle.

"Maybe. I appreciate it all the same." Her mother shut the door, and Grace doubled over in laughter.

"You're so bad," she said.

"Sorry. I really couldn't resist. Every time I see that woman I want to squeegee her eyelashes." He sighed heavily, and she knew this evening would be torture for him. "We'd better go fulfill our duties. Right?"

"I suppose."

They headed downstairs reluctantly, but she could not stop thinking about that moment she'd spent kissing him—or, as her mother had called it, canoodling him. It had left her wanting more. So much more.

What she had to remember was to keep it light, easy and fun. That way she wouldn't get attached, and if she didn't get attached, she wouldn't be hurt when it was over. That was the promise they had made to each other—not to complicate stuff.

So instead she focused on how she was going to make out with him this evening without anyone else hearing. It was kind of titillating to play the rebel child for once, instead of the one who never took risks so they wouldn't ever be a burden again.

It was hard to keep their hands off each other that night, but they did, because she really didn't want her parents to overhear their boisterous lovemaking. And they would have, because she was loud with Jonah. It was freeing to let loose like that.

Life isn't just about sex.

That niggling thought kept playing in the back of her mind.

And as she watched her sister get into her wedding dress, their mother fawning over her, Grace felt a bit sad that she'd never gotten to have this moment.

Or even wanted it, until now.

It hit her that she'd never had those kind of dreams, not real tangible ones, about Victor and her when they were dating.

She'd always expected if they didn't break up, they'd get married; when that hadn't happened she'd given up and had thought she was fine with it. She didn't need a fairy-tale ending.

But now, with Jonah...

She'd been enjoying herself, but there was a part of her that wanted more, and she wanted that something more with him.

She didn't want that court date, and she hated that it was coming up fast.

She didn't want this marriage to end, but she really didn't know how to get the words out, to tell him that she was falling for him and that she kind of wanted something deeper. Forever.

Jonah didn't want any of this. He'd had it before and made it pretty clear he wouldn't do the whole wedding thing again.

This, these feelings of rejection, of hurt, were exactly what she'd been afraid of for so long.

Her sister was beaming, glowing, and Grace was so happy for her.

"Well?" Melanie asked. "You're really quiet."

"You look beautiful, Melanie," Grace remarked, giving her sister a quick hug so as not to wrinkle her wedding dress.

"Thanks! You know, you and Jonah could just do a vow renewal," Melanie hinted.

"Why?" Grace asked.

"So you can wear the dress. You seem so far away, and I just figured you were sad about missing out," Melanie remarked. "Or is something else wrong?"

It was the way her sister said that, as if she was expecting Grace to steal this moment away. Something Grace tried so hard never to do. Her sister, even after all these years later, still struggled with what had happened when they were kids.

It annoyed her, but she swallowed that frustration down. Now was not the time and place to dredge it all up.

"Nothing else is wrong," she lied. "You're right. That's it. I wanted to wear the dress. Kind of hard to do when you're that drunk."

Melanie laughed, and then the photographer had them pose to take a sister photograph. Grace plastered on her best smile. Only she didn't feel like smiling at all.

"It's time," the wedding coordinator said, peeking into the bridal room. "Everything is set up outside."

Their mom was tearing up as she futzed with Melanie's veil. Their dad came in, and Grace watched as he kissed Melanie on the cheek. Grace had thought she never wanted any of this, especially after Victor had shattered her trust, but now she was envious of it and felt bad for being so selfish, for wanting her own happily-ever-after.

"Let's go," Rick said, and then he smiled and winked at her.

Grace took a deep breath and headed up the stairs to meet the groomsman she was walking with. Thankfully, she hadn't been paired up with Victor. The maid of honor had that pleasure. As she passed through the country club and then out onto the small green clearing where the seats were set up, she kept telling herself to smile and keep smiling so that no one would know what was going on.

She walked down the aisle, seeing where she was supposed to line up for the ceremony, and saw Travis standing there, patiently waiting for Melanie.

It was then, as she walked toward the front that she saw Jonah in the front row next to her little brother, Aidan. He looked so handsome in his suit. Their gazes locked, and this time the fake smile he used around her family and strangers turned real. Her heart melted. She anchored herself to him in that moment.

Yes. She wanted this with him.

They were already married, thanks to too much scotch and bad karaoke, and that was fine. What she wanted was for nothing to change, to end. She wanted their *one day at a time* to go on forever. And that was a scary thought indeed, because she didn't see how it could be possible.

Jonah liked that he had been able to sleep next to Grace last night, but what he hated was that *sleeping* had been all they did. When he'd gotten back from taking Aunt Gert and her fifteen pounds of mascara home, Grace had been busy until late at night with wedding stuff.

And it had been mentally exhausting playing nice with everyone, without any down time. He had tried to help where he could, but it had been clear he wasn't much use. So by the time Grace had come to bed, she'd just curled beside him and he'd held her. It had been nice, and he'd relaxed. It had felt right.

The past two weeks had been so magical. There were no expectations. He just loved spending time with her. He couldn't remember the last time he'd felt this at peace.

And that had just firmly solidified his resolve: He was falling in love with her. He didn't really want to admit that, even to himself, but as much as he tried to fight it, it was a losing battle. He was falling for her.

And now here she was, walking down the aisle in that strapless teal bridesmaid gown that clashed a bit with her pink hair. She was the most breathtaking woman in the bridal party He lost his breath for one moment and had a flare of possessive jealousy at the groomsman who got to usher her down the aisle.

It made him a bit sad that they hadn't gotten that.

He'd seen what they did get on that terrible, lopsided, blurry video at the wedding chapel. It had been nothing like this. And Grace deserved a moment like this. She deserved it all. He just wasn't sure he could give it to her.

When their gazes locked, it was like time had no meaning and all he could see was her. Eventually, she moved to the front and stood next to the other bridesmaids. Melanie came out on her father's arm, but Jonah didn't see her. She was Travis's. All he saw was Grace, this woman that he was falling in love with.

His partner, who was becoming his best friend.

What sobered him up was—what if he lost all that?

They'd talked about this. Forever wasn't part of the plan. Honestly, Jonah really had a hard time believing that if he made any move in that direction, all this goodness, this love wouldn't be snatched away from him. He'd thought that he and Mona were going to last forever when they were first married, and that had ended. Then he'd thought that he and Justin would be best friends forever, until Justin had died. In his own weird little way, he'd thought he would have his parents forever too, but now they were gone. He hadn't been ready for them to leave him so soon, even if logically, their ages made it a foregone conclusion.

Forever wasn't sustainable. It wasn't reality, and it hurt to lose and lose and be alone. He'd gotten so used to only relying on himself. It had been easier this way, but as he watched Grace up at the altar, standing outside on a beautiful summer twilight, the red rocks of the cliffs in St. George gleaming brightly against the green of the golf course, he didn't want to be alone any longer.

He just wanted forever with her, and it terrified him because he didn't know how to reach out and take it. He wasn't sure if she wanted him back.

Melanie and Travis were married. It was beautiful. Everyone was happy and cheered. It was apparent to Jonah that they were in love. After the wedding ceremony came the pictures. As Jonah walked away, he was accosted by Aunt Gert to be a part of the family photo.

His stomach sank to his feet as he was dragged out onto the green to where Grace's family was standing.

"Found him," Aunt Gert announced.

"I thought your eyesight was bad," Jonah teased her half-heartedly. He couldn't let himself get so lost in his thoughts. He couldn't let Grace's family see this side of him. He had to put on a brave face.

Aunt Gert shrugged and blinked a couple of times. "You're easy to spot, Mr. Cute Paramedic."

Grace choked back a laugh and came over. "Thanks, Aunt Gert."

Aunt Gert waved and meandered off to get in a photo with the bride.

"I don't think I should be here," Jonah whispered under his breath.

"Yes, you should."

"Grace, but this…"

"I know, but it would look weird if you weren't. It'll be okay. I'm going to take the blame for this whole thing when it ends. I'll tell them that I coerced you." She dragged him by the arm over to where the photos were being taken, but all he could think about was what she said, how she would take the blame when this whole thing ended.

Which meant that she was planning for the end.

Here he was thinking about their future, but

she was already looking ahead to the end. It saddened him, but what had he expected? And as he stood and listened to the photographer pose them for the photographs, he couldn't help but feel like he shouldn't be in the pictures. He really didn't belong here. He didn't belong anywhere.

He was alone after all.

You don't have to be. Tell her. Convince her.

Only he couldn't. His heart was breaking and it was all his fault, but as he looked down at Grace, he was still glad he'd taken the risk. Even though he'd never planned on falling in love again, he had.

He was so in love with her.

It was going to be hard when the end came, but he knew one thing: If their marriage ended and they just went back to being the way they'd been before, that wouldn't be enough for him. He would always want more when it came to Grace.

He couldn't exist where she was around and not love her, not have her in his life. Friendship wasn't enough.

So when their marriage ended, he would accept defeat and move on to another place. He would have to leave Las Vegas, because try as he might to hold it back, his heart was most definitely on the line. It belonged to her.

But he wasn't sure if her heart belonged to him, and he was terrified to find out the answer.

CHAPTER ELEVEN

SOMETHING HAD CHANGED. Jonah had been acting a bit aloof after her sister's marriage ceremony. Grace thought everything had been okay. The way he had been so flirty with her the night before and then the way he'd looked at her when she walked down the aisle gave her the impression of a man in love, but the moment that Aunt Gert had brought him over for family photos, everything had changed.

He'd become closed off, quiet.

She sensed something had shifted between them, but she wasn't sure what. Now he was sitting with her family during the wedding reception and seemed to be enjoying himself enough. She was stuck at the head table and wishing she was sitting with him so they could talk, joke, laugh.

When she was with him, she was always having a good time, and there was no one at the head table she particularly wanted to make small talk with. When she'd first started to really get to know Jonah that had been something they both had in common: They loathed idle chitchat. He was just so much better at faking it than she was.

Jonah wore a mask in order to be social. She'd thought the rapport between them had been real, but now she wasn't so sure.

After the dinner the emcee announced Melanie and Travis for the first time as man and wife. Travis took his bride out on the ballroom floor as they slow danced to their first song. Grace's heart longed to share that moment with Jonah.

When the first dance was over, her father got up to the podium to make a speech.

"Welcome, everyone. If you don't know me, I'm Rick Landon, father of the bride, and the amazing and generous man buying your dinner tonight."

There was a faint titter of laughter.

"Leslie and I are so glad to have Travis as part of the family. I thought I was only gaining one son-in-law this year, but I've been blessed with two."

Grace's stomach turned as her dad mentioned her at Melanie's wedding. Jonah smiled tightly and looked at her. She knew he was struggling with the marriage charade again. Honestly, she was too, and she wanted to tell her parents the truth. But now was not the time and place. Her father finished his speech with a lot of funny jokes about Travis and Melanie, about golf.

Once the speeches by the parents were over, the

dance floor opened up to everyone. Finally Grace was able to get up and away from the head table, from her duties as a bridesmaid and spend some time with Jonah and find out what was wrong.

"Hey," she greeted him, coming up behind his chair. He was sitting alone, as the rest of the family was either out dancing or mingling.

"Hi," he responded quietly.

"Dinner okay?" She leaned forward. "Aunt Gert freaking you out?"

Jonah chuckled softly. "It's fine."

"Fine? That's all you have to say?"

"I'm..." He trailed off and laughed. "I was going to say *fine* again, but I didn't think you'd accept that."

"Probably not. Why don't we dance?" Logically she knew they needed to talk, but this wasn't the place to do that. All she wanted was to be with him.

Jonah nodded and took her hand, leading her out onto the dance floor. He pulled her in close, but not as tight as he did last night in her room. He was holding back, and it was worrying Grace.

Again she had to ask herself what had changed.

His behavior reminded her of Victor. He'd started acting this way right before she'd found out he'd cheated on her. Back then she had sensed something was wrong, but she'd pushed it all aside, telling herself back then that they were happy. She'd gone out of her way to please him.

It turned out they hadn't been happy, or at least he hadn't been, and everyone had known that he'd been having the affair with Nancy. And she'd felt so small after.

This time, she didn't want to ignore the obvious signs that something was wrong.

If things were going to end, she wanted to be the first to know and go into it with her head held high.

Things are going to end though, she reminded herself. *That's the plan.*

She was getting too carried away by all these wedding emotions. That had to be it.

"You seem distracted. And don't say you're fine, because I can tell you're not."

Jonah sighed. "Okay, you caught me. I'm not."

"What's up?"

"It was the photos. I shouldn't have been in them."

"Why?" And it was a silly question, really. She knew why, but there was also a part of her that believed he did belong in those photographs with her family.

With her.

"You said so yourself, in a way. You said that you'll take the blame when this ends. Are you already planning for the end?"

It was a blunt question and to the point. Grace swallowed the lump in her throat as they slowly danced. "We have a court date. I was just stating a fact."

"Enough about the court date," he snapped. "You don't have to shoulder this whole thing yourself. We're both to blame. My problem is I don't know how much longer this can go on."

It was the truth, although it stung.

Time really was ticking away.

"You're right. We'll tell them tomorrow."

Jonah's spine stiffened. "Okay."

"You still don't seem like you *are* okay though."

"No. I'm not. I thought…" He cursed under his breath and then nervously expelled air. "I wish your dad hadn't included me in his speech."

"I didn't know he was going to do that," she said softly.

And it was still eating away at her that her father had done that, had centered her for a second at Melanie's wedding.

Jonah relaxed and held her a little tighter, almost like he didn't want to let her go. "I really like them."

Only them? her little insecure voice asked, but she didn't ask that out loud.

"They like you too."

He nodded. "I just thought…"

"Thought what?" Her heart was beating so fast, it felt like it was going to sprout wings and leave her body. Maybe he wanted more too.

Maybe he did want her.

She was going to tell him she didn't want this to end. Yes, they had to tell her parents the truth about their fake marriage, but she wanted to make this relationship real. She wanted to make this work. Being married to her partner and best friend would be a dream.

Because yeah, he was becoming her best friend. It had been a long time since she'd let someone come into her life and take up that role.

"When it ends, I think I need to leave Vegas," Jonah said.

Grace blinked a couple of times. "Leave Vegas?"

He nodded, not looking at her. "It's for the best."

"Is it?"

"Don't you think?" he questioned.

First, she felt a bit dumbstruck, then angry at herself for thinking this could be more. Why had she thought it could be different, that things would change?

When really they couldn't.

She should've known better.

She opened her mouth to say more when his phone began to buzz.

He pulled it out of his pocket and frowned. "It's work."

"What?" she asked, because she didn't have her phone on her. She glanced back at the table where her little bag was; her sister was motioning that her phone was vibrating too. "What do they say?"

"We're being called back to the station house. Right away. They're forecasting extreme flash flooding tomorrow. Apparently, a huge storm is bringing in monsoon rain from the southeast. All emergency services are being called in. We're officially on active duty."

She was still reeling over the fact he was going to leave Las Vegas, that he was running away.

"We'd better go."

She wanted to stay here and talk with Jonah. She wanted to solve this uncertainty tonight, but there was no time. They both put their jobs first, and right now her priorities lay with work. First, she had to tell her family she had to leave.

She moved toward the table where Melanie sat, then turned to look back at Jonah with longing. He looked a little defeated.

Grace's stomach sank into an anxious little knot. Something indeed had changed and not for the better, but after this emergency was over she was going to make it right. She was going to protect her heart and let him go.

The rain had been coming down steadily since they'd arrived back at the station house to report and change into their uniforms. They'd just left the wedding with what they'd had on them, because they could get their suitcases later. Grace had put on her flashing light that she carried in her car so that local state troopers and highway patrol would know that they were emergency services and on their way to active duty.

As they'd left the country club, the emergency warnings had started pinging on their phones; St. George had been put on a flash-flood warning too. The storm was not seasonal and highly unusual. The desert did see its fair share of flash floods and mudslides, but this was excessive.

Jonah was worried about how Grace was doing. He knew how she felt about water.

Not much had been said on the long car ride down, and he'd been fine with that. At least he'd gotten a chance to tell her that he was going to leave. She hadn't really reacted, which just reaffirmed that he'd made the right decision.

Except it didn't feel that way.

It frustrated him.

He'd wanted a reaction from her. He'd wanted her to fight for him to stay, wanted a chance to fight for her too.

Maybe he was just tired of locking everything he was feeling away. It had been easier for him to do that in the past to cope with everything, to protect himself, but it was exhausting.

It was tiring trying to hide how he felt about her.

Now was not the time to have all these big feelings. He worked hard to lock them all down. He had to focus on the task at hand.

He had never seen rain like this. Almost as

soon as the storm hit, they'd started getting calls for the emergency services. There had been no time to evacuate the low-lying areas.

The fire department, who they shared a station with, was just as busy as they were. He and Grace were running on a lot of strong coffee and adrenaline. The station had the local news playing in the background as they covered the storm and tried to give updates the best they could. There were power fluctuations as the wind brought down power lines.

"It's like a hurricane," John mumbled under his breath. He'd just gotten back in from a call and needed to change as his uniform was soaked.

Grace tilted her head, half listening.

"Is it?" Jonah asked. "I've never been in a hurricane before."

"This is like it. Same pressure changes, the wind. It's all similar. I'm from Louisiana originally. There will be flooding. Be prepared for that," John stated morosely. "Drownings. It'll be awful."

Grace sat up straight, and Jonah knew that she was worrying about that. All he wanted to do was go over and comfort her, but he held back, because they'd never shown an unrestrained amount of affection at work and that was what they both wanted. She most likely would push him away.

"Hey, Crandall and Landon. Call out on the highway heading to Henderson. Flooding. People trapped and the road is washed out. We need an extra rig down there."

Grace nodded, but he could tell by her tight expression she was worried. "Come on, Crandall."

Jonah mirrored her nod, and they made their way to their rig.

"You going to be okay?"

"Fine," Grace remarked. Only he wasn't too sure about that.

Everything was loaded with what they needed. They pulled on their rain gear, and the ambulance bay door opened. The moment it opened, the wind drove the rain in driving pellets against the rig, and as they pulled out onto the road he could barely hear the siren over the roaring of the wind.

The wind was gusting so strong, the rig was shaking.

Grace's jaw was set with determination, her knuckles white from gripping the steering wheel as she headed out into the storm.

"Hey," Jonah said.

She barely glanced at him. "I know. This will be okay."

"We've got this, partner."

She looked at him quickly, her shoulders easing slightly. "Let's go save lives, yes?"

He grinned. "Yes."

What was usually a short drive dragged on as they dodged traffic and detours. There were many roads that were already overflowing. Reservoirs used to divert flooding were streaming fast with muddy water, and yet the rain was still coming.

There were flashes of light mixed with low rumbles of thunder, but the loudest was the howling wind. People had been caught unawares; no one expected part of the highway to wash away, especially not in the desert.

Grace pulled up where there were already a cluster of flashing lights from the fire department, police and rescue. She parked the rig, and Jonah had to fight the wind to open the door and head out into the driving rain.

It pelted at his skin, and it was cold.

It stung like a thousand knives.

He glanced over at her. Her expression was unreadable, but he knew she was feeling stressed. She was facing her biggest fear.

As they got out of the ambulance the police chief came over. "Thank goodness. We're having a hell of a time. There's people trapped in cars. We have a rope, but no one is small enough to get in through that sunroof. We get there and we sink it further as we try to make the hole larger."

"I can fit," Grace said with determination.

Jonah's eyes widened. He wanted to protest, but the police chief just nodded. "Yeah, it looks like you might. Let's get you tied up."

Grace nodded nervously.

Jonah couldn't let her do this. What if she froze and got hurt? Or worse...

It was the "worse" that he couldn't even begin to fathom. It terrified him to his core.

Echoes of blasts and scents of the tunnel from his time overseas washed over him.

Only this time it was Grace broken in his arms, not Justin. And picturing that made his stomach turn. It made him want to cry out, a silent scream that welled up deep inside of him.

There was no way he could let her take the risk. To lose her would kill him. "Let me."

Grace turned toward him. She was clearly frustrated. "I can do this."

"Can you? That's fast water. It'll be deep."

"I can do my job," she replied firmly. "Don't speak for me or presume."

Jonah wanted to stop her, hold her back, but he knew that he couldn't. What right did he have? She wasn't his.

Isn't she?

"You're not going to die."

"No, I'm not. Why would you think that?"

She turned to leave, but he grabbed her, too frantic to stop himself. It was happening all over again. The panic, the idea of losing someone he loved. It felt like he was spiraling out of control. Getting close to her had not been good for him.

"No, I won't let you."

"It's my job," she shouted. "A partner wouldn't stop me."

"I'm your husband!"

Her eyes widened. "Are you really my husband? Really?"

The truth was he wasn't. She'd made it clear the end of their relationship was coming, and he'd told her he would be leaving Vegas. Seeing her here amid all this danger should've just strengthened his resolve to move on, yet he couldn't.

He didn't want to.

And it was too scary to be vulnerable to her, to stay in spite of it all and fight for what he really wanted.

Always he'd taken the easy way out, the path of least resistance. It was simpler to do it that way instead of expressing himself.

Is it really easy though?

There was a part of him, buried down so deep and locked away, that wanted to tell her why he couldn't let her risk her life like that. That he wouldn't be able to bear it if he lost her, like he'd lost Justin.

Only he couldn't find the words. It was too hard to say what he wanted to say. That he loved her. That he'd fallen in love with her and wanted more and needed her to know that, even if she didn't want the same.

She'd already made it clear at her sister's wedding that she was done, that she was ready to move on.

Telling her how he felt—that he wasn't ready to move on, never would be—would just drive her further away, destroy what was left of their friendship and take Jonah with it.

He could feel the anxiety rising in him. All he wanted to do was run, run from the possible pain of losing her. His heart was breaking in two.

This was too much.

This was too hard.

Coward.

"Well?" she asked.

He didn't say anymore. There was nothing he could say. She wasn't his, and he had to let her go.

She pulled away from him, slipped out of his fingers and went with the rescue crews to get a harness on.

There were people being pulled out of the water, and he had no time to watch her, he had no time to entertain his terror of her going out there and putting her life on the line or the real possibility he'd lose her.

Instead, he took the patients as they were brought to them and got them safe, dry and was assessing them for their medical needs as more ambulance sirens were being pulled into the site from all the different directions.

Only once did he glance back to see her with the emergency-rescue team. She was standing at the edge of the water receiving instructions, and then she was going, wading out into the flood and making her way to that semi-submerged car.

In that moment, he knew what he wanted, and he was done being scared or worried about it all.

Grace was facing her biggest fear to save a life. She wasn't taking the easy way out or making an excuse not to try something she was afraid of. Neither should he. Even if she didn't feel the same about him, he wanted her to know what he truly thought of her, how much she deserved happiness.

She was worthy of love. She was brave and kind and good.

She was everything, and he had to let her know. He had to take the chance and stop running from his emotions. It was time to be brave just like her.

He didn't want to lose her like he'd lost Justin. But he didn't want to push her away like he had Mona either. For so long he'd spent so much time trying to bury the horrors of that last mission, of losing Justin, that he really was spending his time pushing everyone away to regain control of his life. It had been safer that way, but what kind of life had it been?

Since he had married Grace and agreed to fake their relationship, his life had finally become worth living again and it was just hitting him now. All this time, for so many years he had just been existing.

And it hadn't been much of that.

Now, watching her on the precipice of something dangerous, something that he knew would absolutely push her to the limits, there were so many things he wanted to say to her. Suddenly it was all just rushing to come out of him. It wasn't the time. They had their work to do. Lives depended on them.

He was proud of her as she took this chance.

He just hoped that he hadn't missed *his* chance and that the woman he loved wouldn't be swept away by the currents before he had a chance to make things right, to tell her how much she meant to him. How incredible she was, how she deserved to be happy.

Even if that happiness wouldn't be with him.

CHAPTER TWELVE

Breathe. Just breathe.

Usually when Grace attended near drownings the person had already been pulled to safety, or at the very least they were in a pool that didn't have currents, other than the usual jets that circulated water. Once she had had to go into the Bellagio fountains, but the display had been turned off while they handled that emergency.

This was a first for her.

She was scared, but she'd been attached to a guide rope and had a life jacket on. The water was rushing like a torrent, and it was rising as the rain continued to come down. Before she stepped out into the water, she looked back to see Jonah helping those they had pulled out of the water.

Their gazes briefly locked in that moment, and she knew he was scared for her. She'd been frustrated when he tried to stop her, like what she was doing was foolish or selfish.

This was her job.

A terrifying part of it, but this was what she'd signed up for when she became a paramedic.

When he'd said he was her husband, for one moment she'd felt some hope, but he hadn't said anything else and she knew he was just saying whatever he could to keep her safe.

She knew Jonah had been thinking about Justin then. She could see it in his eyes that he was comparing her to his long-dead best friend.

It should have been touching, but instead the reminder stung. That was what he thought of her. A friend.

Nothing more.

He'd confirmed it. He didn't love her enough to claim the title of *husband*.

It hurt. Just like when he told her he was leaving. As if being married to her had become a burden. So much so that he had to leave Vegas entirely, and she doubted there was anything she could do to make him stay.

And did she really want him to stay because of an obligation?

No.

She didn't want that. It hurt even more to force her heart to accept that.

"You ready?" The rescue chief shouted over the wind, interrupting her morose thoughts.

Grace nodded and gave a thumbs-up. She stepped out into the water. The current was strong, and she wasn't sure what debris would be under her feet. With each step she took she was trying to picture the freeway underneath her, but there were cars and other things being pushed and rocked and washed over the roadway.

You've got this. You're safe.

The car that was her target was about three hundred feet away. She could see the top of the woman's head and an arm as she tried to pull herself up and out of the sunroof. It was a small opening, and the car was already leaning heavily as the water rushed against it.

Another set of emergency workers were on the far side; they were closer to the car, but they had more obstacles between them and it. They were sending someone out too to help her. Grace knew without a doubt the woman trapped inside most likely was hypothermic, had probably swallowed a lot of dirty water and might have injuries that were unknown. She would die if they didn't get there soon.

She was smaller than the other EMTs on the scene and hopefully could traverse the precarious car to get the woman out. On her back she had the Jaws of Life—a hydraulic ram and cutter, so that she could make the opening wider if she needed to.

As she stepped closer, her ankle rolled on a rock or something and she slipped. The line tightened and there was shouting, but she wasn't sure if that was the shouting she was hearing from the shoreline or the screaming in her head.

Lock it all away. Focus. I can do this.

She steadied her steps and kept going. The water was getting higher than her waist, and it felt like she might be swept away. Her pulse was racing, filling her ears with the thundering beats, but she kept her eyes locked on that car. There was an EMT standing there, but every time he tried to get close, the car would shift under his weight.

Eyes still locked on the top of the woman's head and that one pale arm that was clinging on for dear life, Grace made it to the car.

"Glad you're here. She's fading," the rescue worker stated. "Every time I put any weight on it, the car gives and shifts. I can hold it, and you can climb up there. Her seat belt has lashed her down."

Grace nodded as the rescue worker braced the car with a pole he had. The two EMTs who were coming from the other side had a backboard. If they got the woman out, the four of them could get that backboard through the obstacles and to the far side. Although she wasn't sure how far her guide rope would let her go. She would probably have to back track.

She slowly climbed onto the car. It was rocking and swaying, but it wasn't tilting under her weight, not with the other rescue worker using a ram to hold it steady. Water began to bubble and froth as the intensity increased.

"My name is Grace. I'm here to help," Grace shouted at the woman.

"Janice," she woman slurred. "I'm stuck and so tired."

"I know. Just hold on, okay." Grace did a quick assessment of the woman. There was definite laceration, and it looked like her shoulder was dislocated. Grace pulled out the Jaws of Life.

They were small and portable, but they were gas powered and could still exert enough pounds of pressure to widen the sunroof and allow her to cut the seat belt that was holding the patient captive. As Grace quickly took in the situation, she was pretty sure that the seat belt was the only reason why the woman hadn't been washed away. Before she released that, she would have to have the woman hooked on to the harness she carried, or she would be carried away with the current.

Grace worked fast to get the harness around the woman's torso and had it secured to her.

"Janice, I need you to hold on tight like you have been. Nod once if you understand."

Janice nodded weakly. "Hurry. I can't feel my legs."

Grace used the cutter and the ram, spreading

open the sunroof enough to allow her to slip her hand down and grab hold of the seat belt.

"Hold tight, Janice," Grace shouted as she cut the seat belt. There was a whoosh, and water came spilling out the opened broken window.

"Got her?" The EMT bracing the car asked. "The car is moving."

"Got her," Grace yelled. She used her strength, bracing against the metal as she pulled the woman up and out of the sunroof. Grace was only five foot eight; Janice was at least five foot ten and a complete dead weight. Her other arm was at an angle, so there were definitely broken bones.

The other two EMTs had arrived and helped stabilize the car as they got Janice down and strapped onto the backboard. Grace repacked the Jaws of Life and clambered down off the wreckage. She helped get Janice clear and then got out of the way as Janice's car was pushed completely over.

"Christ! We need to get out of here," the first EMT shouted. The other two had started off toward safety on their side, carrying Janice on the backboard between them.

"Yes, I agree. Have we got everyone from the cars?" Grace asked.

"She was the last."

They both started making the walk back to their side. She could see the other two rescue workers had managed to get Janice through their obstacles and she would get the help she needed, which was a relief.

Now she had to get back and help Jonah with the patients on their side.

The water continued to rise, but she kept her eyes locked on her rig, because she knew that was where Jonah was. They might not have had a real relationship, but it was grounding to know he was there. He was her friend, after all.

In her heart, though, she knew that wasn't enough. Not really. She wanted more, so much more that it felt like she was going to break into a million pieces when she thought about him leaving. She swallowed the lump in her throat and fought back the tears as she focused on getting back safely. The rain became harder, and it was getting even more difficult to see. The wind picked up, and she was being thrashed around.

Every step was like she was walking through thick cement. It was exhausting.

"Almost there!" the EMT ahead of her screamed over the roar of water and thunder.

Grace nodded, not that he saw it, but she was getting cold and tired too.

Something hit her then, causing white-hot burning pain to shoot down her side. It dug into her skin, causing her suit to tear, and her life jacket was ripped away. She screamed in agony, and her arm went limp.

"Grace!" someone shouted from the shoreline.

She was jolted again, this time losing her footing.

Oh, God.

All she could do was grab the rope and hold on as the water came tumbling over her head and she was swept underneath.

Jonah had come back around to the front of the rig after treating a patient and getting them loaded up in another rig that had come to collect them. He couldn't drive anywhere until Grace got back, because she might have that last victim with her.

He saw that Grace and the other rescue worker were coming back from the water. On the far side of the flow, he saw the patient she had saved from the wreckage was being taken care of. He let out a breath of relief that he hadn't even known he'd been holding. He watched as Grace followed the guide rope back toward solid ground.

Then he saw the surge, the rubble that was coming directly for them.

Internally, he screamed and then shouted out, hoping that he'd been heard, but it was hard over the rush of water.

The largest piece of deadwood, from what looked like an old cattle fence, hit Grace in the side. She cried out and winced; it knocked her backward.

He ran for the water but was held back by John, who had just arrived on scene.

"You can't," John said firmly. "The surge is too high."

"She'll drown!" Jonah was wracked with worry, with grief. There was nothing he could do in this moment but watch. He was powerless with Justin, and he was powerless here too. And he'd wasted his chance to tell her how he felt, that he loved her. His fear had held him back, and he'd blown it. In that moment he dropped to his knees, taking John down with him. It was all too much, too gut-wrenchingly horrifying.

There was another surge, and the rescue worker ahead of Grace was pulled to shore. He was cut and battered.

John let go of Jonah and rushed to help him.

It was then that Grace disappeared under the torrent of water.

"Pull harder!" the police chief shouted out.

The winch was winding hard, but it appeared she was snagged on something,

"Harness me up. I'm going out!" Jonah screamed. There was no way he could let her die. He wasn't going to lose her this way.

He was harnessed up then and attached to a winch. She wasn't far out, and he followed her rope, which was taught. The water was gurgling and bubbling where he'd last seen her. He didn't have much time to get to her, but he wasn't going to let her drown again.

Not on his watch.

He made it and then reached down into the water, trying to keep his own head above the swell, and found her. He used a knife and cut the straps of the Jaws of Life, which had gotten entangled on something, pinning her down. Once she was free, he brought her head above water and lashed her to his harness.

"I've got you, Grace. I'm here. Don't you damn well die on me."

She was unconscious still, and he had to not think about the worst-possible outcome as he picked up her lifeless body in his arms and carried her to shore. She was bleeding profusely from a large laceration to her arm.

Once he was there, he laid her on the ground and started CPR, pumping on her chest and blowing into her mouth, trying to bring her back. Out of the corner of his eyes he saw an AED had been brought out.

"Breathe, Grace. Breathe!"

He blew into her mouth again, and this time there was a sputter and she spewed out the dark dirty water, gasping and coughing.

Thank God.

"Grace," he murmured.

"Again. Seriously?" she asked weakly.

He smiled at her. "We've got to get you to the hospital and get antibiotics into you. That water is dirty."

Grace nodded. "I'm so cold."

"I know." He touched her face gently and stood back as he let the other paramedics work to get her up on a gurney so they could take her to the hospital.

"Jonah," she called out.

He came to her side. "I'm here."

"I'm sorry. I won't be a burden." She passed out again, only for a moment, groaning.

"You need to go with her," John said. "We'll take care of the rig. Go with your wife."

"She wasn't supposed to be my wife."

John laughed. "I know—I was there that night. But she's your wife now. Go with her."

Jonah nodded and followed the paramedics from another station into the back of the ambulance. They were hooking up a fluid line, and Grace had an oxygen mask on. Her O2 stats were still low, and she probably still had fluid in her lungs.

She was barely conscious as another paramedic wrapped up her arm.

Jonah took a seat next to her.

She blinked a few times and looked at him. "What're you doing?"

"Going with you."

"You don't need to. I can take care of myself."

"I'm here."

"For now." She winced. "I don't need you here. I won't be a burden to you. Don't worry about me."

"Do you want him to leave?" asked Jose, the paramedic attending her, slightly confused.

Grace didn't answer as she drifted off into unconsciousness again.

Jose looked at him. "Thought you two were married?"

"We are, but waiting for a divorce." Saying it out loud gave it a finality that he really didn't like.

"Then maybe you should go," Jose suggested.

"No. I'll make sure she gets there."

She might not have wanted him—not like that—but he cared for her and she was alive.

That was all that mattered.

He sent a silent prayer to whatever deity was listening to him. Just a thanks to the universe and karma, whatever, that she was still here.

She was still here even if she wasn't his. He had a second chance to tell her how he felt. He hadn't lost her like he'd lost Justin.

Close call, doofus.

Jonah couldn't hold back an exhausted grin. That was what Justin would have said if he were here now—Jonah could almost hear his voice in his head.

Only you would this happen to. Only you would

get drunk and marry someone in Vegas and then fall in love with them.

Justin would always tease Jonah about like that. Call him a wiener or a doofus. All those good-natured ribbings that would then turn into roughhousing. It was the first time in a long time that he'd thought of Justin and it hadn't been tainted with guilt and sorrow, just golden memories of joy and fun.

Usually, Jonah would lock all those memories away because he wanted to be able to control his emotions and not let his past affect his work. Right now, he basked in them. It was as though Justin was there, in that moment, reaffirming that there was no need to be afraid.

The ambulance was closed up, and he strapped himself in for the ride to the hospital. Once they got there and he was sure that Grace was stabilized and well taken care of, he had a few phone calls to make.

He had to let her parents know what had happened. Then he was going to tell Grace how he felt, even if she didn't feel the same. She had the right to know. She deserved to know. All of it. Every detail.

And once that was all taken care of, he'd say goodbye to Vegas and to his heart.

But what if you don't have to?

CHAPTER THIRTEEN

Grace was in and out of consciousness, but she was aware of one thing: She hadn't been put on life support. She had a nasal cannula, but that didn't bother her. What bothered her was the fact that she was being put on antibiotics for a while and then she would have to go in to have surgery. When the log or wood hit her arm, it had sliced into her nerves, causing damage, which meant she would be off work for some time.

At least, that was what she thought was happening.

The antibiotics and the painkillers were making her woozy, and she was having a hard time keeping it all straight. She also swore she saw Victor in the room at one point.

She woke up again and glanced over at the small recliner chair, hoping she'd see Jonah but didn't. She didn't know why she'd expected to. He made it clear that their partnership was over; he was leaving. She couldn't blame him. Not really.

She'd almost drowned again, and now her arm

was useless. Once again she'd ignored advice and put her life on the line. She should've listened to Jonah.

She was a burden, and that was the last thing she ever wanted.

A tear slipped out of the corner of her eye. Why couldn't she have just told him she loved him? Why did she have to be such a coward? It was too late, and now he was gone.

There was a knock at the door, and her heart skipped a beat.

It was her parents.

When Grace saw her mother's face, she just broke down in tears because she'd seen that haggard look before and she hated that she'd put her mother through that all again.

"Grace," her mother said, choking back a sob and rushing to her. "Oh, God, Grace."

"I know," Grace said, her voice shaking. "I did it again."

"Honey, when Jonah called us..." Her dad trailed off, and even though he wasn't the kind of man to show emotions, she knew he was fighting back tears. "I'm so glad you're still here."

"I won't be golfing for some time," Grace said, sniffling.

"I don't care about that," her dad said, brushing her hair back. "You're here."

Grace suddenly realized what her dad had said.

"Wait, did you say Jonah called you?" she asked, confused.

"Why wouldn't he?" her mother asked.

"I guess…" Grace trailed off, not sure of what to say. She was surprised he was still there. He'd said he was going to leave.

"You guess what? Of course Jonah called us. He's your husband."

Guilt rolled in the pit of Grace's stomach. After everything else, she'd almost forgotten to dread this conversation. "Mom, Dad… There's something I have to tell you."

"Oh?" her mother asked, taking a seat. "Should we be worried?"

"No, I need to apologize. I lied about my marriage to him."

"You faked that video?" her dad asked, confused.

"No, we really did get married, but we were drunk and it wasn't supposed to happen. We weren't dating. It was a one-night bad choice." Heat flushed her cheeks with embarrassment.

"Oh," her mother said, confused, and yet there was already a hint of disappointment in her voice. "Then why did you lie to me that day? The day I came over?"

Grace swallowed the lump in her throat, a tight knot of emotions threatening to come out of her. All those feelings that she'd kept locked away since she was a child. Everything she had been shouldering for so long. "I couldn't bear to let you down."

Her mother raised her eyebrows. "Let me down?"

"I know I didn't listen to you all those years ago. It was the reason I almost died that day as a child. I know the hospital bills were large, that sacrifices were made because of my mistake. I hid so much from you over the years, because I couldn't face disappointing you that way again."

"You mean like Victor cheating on you?" her dad said tightly, his brow furrowed and his lips thin with what looked like barely controlled anger.

"You knew about that?" Grace asked, stunned.

"Victor came clean when you came into the emergency department unconscious," her dad stated. "I'm only sorry we pushed that relationship on you. He wasn't the right man for you. You deserve more."

"You deserve what you had with Jonah," her mom stated.

"Well, that was all fake."

"Really?" her father questioned. "Didn't seem to be."

"He really seems to care for you," her mother said softly.

"How? I mean… I'm a burden."

"Far from it," her dad interjected.

"Grace, you're not a burden to us. Never." Her mother kissed her on the top of the head.

"You're a people pleaser, and you need to stop smoothing things over with everyone and live your own life," her dad said.

"That's why we're disappointed. Not because you're a burden, but because you can't see how amazing you are," her mom said.

"So you're disappointed now? That the marriage wasn't real?"

"Only because we like Jonah so much." Her mother smiled. "Thank you for telling us the truth. I guess I'm sad because the two of you seem so right for each other. You both seemed so in love."

Her parents were right. She'd lived to long trying to make everyone else happy because she felt so guilty. Her parents, Melanie, Travis, even Victor. Everyone was happy. Everyone got what they wanted, except her.

She wanted to stay married to Jonah. He was part of her life. He'd woven himself in there, and she didn't want that all unraveled. She didn't want to let him go. And in that moment she saw every shared smile, the way he'd looked at her at Melanie's wedding, the touches, the kisses, him showing her how to swim. All their jokes, the laughter and curling up on the couch at night picking terrible movies.

Jonah never wanted her to change or be someone else. With him she could be herself.

Fully and completely.

He was more than a friend and her partner.

He was her everything, and she wasn't going to lose that.

She was going to take a chance on happiness for herself for once.

Once she was discharged, she was going to find him and tell him how she felt. Even if he didn't feel the same way, at least then she would know the truth—and that for once she'd been brave and done everything she could.

She was deserving of a happily-ever-after too, and maybe she could have that fairy tale with Jonah.

There was a knock at the door, and Jonah stuck his head in. There were dark circles under his eyes. A sob caught in her throat, and relief washed though her. All the emotions she'd been holding back came rushing to the surface like a flood.

He was here. He hadn't left.

Her mother kissed Grace's head again and then took her dad's hand, dragging him out of the room. "Let's give these two some privacy."

They slipped out of the room, and it was just the two of them left.

Grace and Jonah.

Alone.

Her heart was racing.

"You're awake," Jonah remarked, coming into the room.

"You've been here the whole time?" she asked, her voice shaking.

He nodded. "In and out."

"You told me you were leaving."

He sighed. "I know. The thing is... I wanted to run, but then, I can't live without you. Watching you face your fears made me realize that. And then seeing you in the water, you almost dying... That killed me."

"I'm sorry."

"I was scared. The thought of you not being there anymore...it was too much." His voice broke, then he took a breath and continued. "The fact is I'm never not going to be scared of losing you, but I'm willing to fight that fear to have you. Grace, I love you."

Grace almost couldn't believe the words she was hearing. Her heart was pounding so hard it had to be spiking the monitor. "I'm scared too," she managed. "The thing is... The thing is I love you as well, Jonah. I was scared to tell you in case you didn't feel the same. I didn't want to make you uncomfortable, but I do love you. I wanted you to know. I have for some time."

He smiled, his eyes twinkling as he lifted her other hand to his lips, placing a kiss against her knuckles. "I love you too, and I don't want our marriage to end. I want to give it a chance. The right way. I want you to be my wife for real."

A tear slid out of the corner of her eyes, relief washing through her. "I want that too."

"Still, it terrified me seeing you go under the water..." He trailed off and then took her hand, squeezing it gently before laughing softly. "Sorry—just had to touch you to convince myself you're still here and you're okay."

"I'm here," she whispered, squeezing his hand back.

"I know. It was the worst moment of my life. I thought I lost you."

"You saved me though," she said gently.

"I was proud of you for overcoming your fear like that."

"It was scary, but I thought back to what you taught me about grounding myself in the water and how I got into all of this to be like the paramedic who saved me, and that's kind of a hard thing to emulate when you're afraid of water. I couldn't let Janice die like that."

"And you didn't. She's going to be fine. She's in this hospital too. Her family is very thankful, but they can come by later. We have to get you ready for surgery. They want to make sure all that dirt and mulch you swallowed under water is out and that your lungs are strong enough to withstand the surgery to repair the nerves."

Grace sighed. "You're going to be without me as a partner for a while."

He nodded. "I can take a few weeks' leave to

take care of you, but yeah, until you're back on the job, I'm working with John."

"John? Oh, boy."

Jonah shrugged. "He's not so bad. He was our wedding videographer, after all."

Grace laughed and held her belly. She felt a bit woozy. "I told my parents, apologized for lying."

"You don't have to shoulder all of the blame. Shall I get them so *we* can apologize and tell them we're staying together?"

"You better."

Jonah leaned over her and kissed her softly on the lips. "You know, I'm not sure how our marriage will work."

"What do you mean?"

"It took a near-death experience for both of us to see sense."

She laughed weakly. "I think it will work. I love you, and I'm willing to work on it if you are. No running away."

He smiled, his eyes twinkling with unshed tears. "Deal. I'm not going anywhere."

He stepped out to get her parents.

Her mom was wringing her hands together as she came in the room. "So?"

"We're staying together," Grace stated as Jonah took her good hand.

"I fell in love with your daughter, and she loves me. We're going to stay married and make this work," Jonah reiterated.

Grace watched her parents' expression soften from confusion to happiness.

"Well, thank goodness! I knew you two would see sense," her mom said.

"I'm sorry I lied to you both. But I truly do love your daughter," Jonah said.

"So, have you lied to me about anything else, Jonah?" her dad asked in a teasing yet stern voice.

"I hate golf. So much," Jonah replied.

They all laughed, and the door opened as a doctor snuck in.

"Hello, everyone. I'm Dr. Page. Grace the hero, I'm glad to see you more alert. The last couple of times I've been by you've been pretty out of it. I want to do an examination on you and then go over some stuff we found from your blood work."

"Do we need to leave?" Grace's dad asked.

"No, it's fine." Dr. Page turned to Jonah. "You're her husband?"

Jonah grinned and then squeezed her hand. "I am."

"Good. I'm glad you're all here. So, we have to do some surgery to repair the damage to the nerve on your arm. You've been on a course of tetracycline to help manage the onset of infection from the containments in the water, but we're going to stop that now."

"Oh?" Grace asked. "Are my lungs clear? They feel kind of heavy still."

"That we don't know. We're going to have to

get an MRI rather than an X-ray now. Just checking with your insurance now."

"Why can't she have an X-ray?" Jonah asked.

"Because of the baby. I wish that had been disclosed when she arrived and before we started the tetracycline," Dr. Page remarked, shooting Jonah a pointed glare. "This is why we always check blood work. Husbands don't always know."

"Baby?" Grace asked, dumbfounded. "I'm pregnant?"

"Six weeks. You didn't know, I take it?" Dr. Page asked, shocked.

"No." Grace glanced over at Jonah. "I was on the pill and... Pregnant?"

"Yes. So we're going to have to change our approach. We need to get the surgery done, but there are still risks involved," Dr. Page continued.

"Okay." She was still processing it all.

A baby had never been part of her plan. She wasn't opposed to the idea; it was just she had never thought it would happen, because she didn't expect to ever have a husband.

Dr. Page stopped one of the intravenous meds. "I'll be back with a change in script, and the surgeon will come by to talk about the surgery. I've also set up a consult with OB-GYN."

"Thank you, Dr. Page," Jonah said. He sounded a bit dumbfounded.

Dr. Page nodded and left the room, and Grace just let it all sink in. She was going to be a mother.

"I'm so happy!" her mother exclaimed. "It was a bit weird at first, with the whole fake marriage, but I'm so thrilled I'm going to be a grandma. Finally!"

"Come on, let's give these two some time to let it sink in," her dad said, pulling her mom away.

When they were alone, Jonah sat down on the edge of the bed.

"What do you think?" she asked with trepidation.

This was not how Jonah had thought today was going to turn out. He'd sat at Grace's bedside for the last twenty-four hours. Ever since he'd realized he couldn't live without her, couldn't leave without letting her know how he felt, he'd been so frightened.

It was scary to love someone so much, to know how much it would hurt if she didn't feel the same.

But saying it had felt good, and hearing her admit that she loved him too had made him ecstatic. And when Dr. Page had announced that Grace was pregnant, Jonah just had to shake his head in disbelief. A long time ago he'd wanted a family, but it had been so off his radar for a long time, something he'd never thought would happen.

Then again, he'd never thought that he would find love and get married again. Here he was, doing everything he'd thought was impossible.

He'd been an idiot for even contemplating running away from this.

He deserved happiness too.

"Jonah, you're not saying much," Grace's voice trembled with trepidation.

"I'm at a loss for words."

"Same." She made a face, one that meant *eek*. "I was on the pill."

"Yeah, but six weeks—that's our wedding night." He ran his hand through his hair. "A honeymoon baby."

"We never really got a honeymoon."

"You get yourself feeling better, and we'll go on a babymoon."

"I'd like to go to California, see where you grew up."

He touched her face, running his fingers across her soft skin, knowing she was still here and his. "Done."

"Not on the back of the bike though."

"Yeah, probably not. How are you feeling about all of this?"

"Scared out of mind, but I'm happy. Are you?"

"Very. Almost losing you—it was too much. I never did think I'd find love again, and honestly after losing Justin like that, I didn't think I deserved to find it. I pushed a lot of people away, and I think, on some level, I was trying to do the same to you."

"I understand that. I was trying to do the same.

I didn't want to be a burden. I just wanted everyone happy, except me, because I didn't think I deserved it either."

"I think we're both dunderheads."

Grace laughed and then coughed. "What?"

"We were both being stubborn and couldn't see what was right in front of us."

"Kind of like Aunt Gert," she teased. "Thick blinders on."

He winced, smiling. "That is true. I'm in love with you, Grace, and though I really wasn't expecting a baby, I'm glad it's with you. I'm glad I'm going to be a family with you. My only regret is my parents aren't here to see it and to know you." He brushed away a tear.

"I wish I'd met them too. You can tell our baby all about them and Justin."

He leaned over and kissed her. "I love you, Mrs. Cute Paramedic."

"I love you too, Mr. Cute Paramedic."

Then he reached down and touched her belly. "And I love Cute Paramedic Junior too."

Grace groaned. "Oh, no, we're not calling them that."

"I hope not."

She worried her bottom lip. "I do have one more request from you."

"Oh?"

"We need to renew our vows. I want to have that experience with you. It can be small, but I don't want our wedding photos and video to be some blurry, drunken thing. I want something real to look back on and for our kids to see."

Jonah chuckled. "*Kids* now?"

"Yes. I want more than one. No more people pleasing. I'm telling you I want three."

"Three?" he laughed. "Maybe I will run."

"I'm not letting you go."

They kissed sweetly. "I'm not letting you go ever. I keep my promises."

"I know."

He kissed her one more time, wanting to hold on to her forever, but she had to rest. There would be time for that when she healed. And it was time that he was looking forward to.

EPILOGUE

BREATHE. JUST BREATHE. And don't kick me so much.

It was probably never really any woman's dream to get married while four months pregnant, but this was way better than Grace's previous wedding. No one was drunk or singing offbeat songs, and the videographer was a hired professional, which had made John a little sad, until Jonah had asked him to stand next to him and Travis at the altar.

It wasn't a real wedding, because she and Jonah had decided to cancel their court date and keep that first marriage legal, but she meant what she'd said when she was in the hospital. She wanted to do it right.

She wanted the dress.

She wanted the small reception, and she wanted that first dance with her husband.

Jonah was agreeable too, as his first wedding had been an elopement.

They did keep it small, even though her mother had wanted to do something big. And Grace had agreed to have it at her parents' country club, just like her sister, Melanie.

Right now, as she stood in the bride's room, she was trying to calm both her nerves and the baby, who was doing backflips in her stomach.

Even though there had been some worry about her surgery to repair the damage done to her arm, she and the baby had come through it all just fine. She did miss work though, and she couldn't wait to get the all-clear.

She'd be on dispatch duty for a while, because she was pregnant, but at least she'd be doing something other than sitting at home.

The baby did another flip, and she reached down to touch her stomach.

"You okay, honey?" her dad asked.

"Just the baby. Kicking me."

"I can't believe you got pregnant before me and married before me too," Melanie chided.

"You're pregnant now too. Besides, I'm the oldest." Grace winked.

Once she was discharged from the hospital and Melanie was back from her honeymoon, Grace went to visit her and have a heart-to-heart. They both agreed it was time for a new beginning.

They both loved each other—they were family, but they wanted a deeper relationship. Now Grace was excited about the future and their new sisterly relationship.

"The question is when are you going to move

to St. George so our kids can grow up together?" Melanie asked.

"Time will tell." Grace smiled secretively, because it was something she and Jonah had been talking about. They both wanted the baby to be close to family, and they were both working on getting transferred in the next year from Nevada to Utah, but she'd miss Vegas.

Vegas was home and had been for some time. Las Vegas had been where she'd had her fairytale realization.

"You ready?" her dad asked.

"Yes. Definitely."

"He's a good man," her dad said. "And I'm glad this time we can be here for it."

"Me too."

Melanie went ahead, and then their dad escorted Grace out to the main room where the family was waiting.

When she saw Jonah at the end of the aisle, all that nervousness floated away.

She hadn't seen him since they'd arrived yesterday. Her mother had been insistent that it was bad luck for him to stay at their place for the night, so he'd gone to stay with Melanie and Travis.

She'd missed him, so seeing him standing there in his tux made her heart flip with anticipation. As soon as the family dinner was over, they were getting into her car and driving to California to spend a couple of weeks traveling around to all

Jonah's old haunts, to visit his parents' resting place and Justin's name carved into the war memorial in his hometown.

Her dad walked her over to Jonah.

"Take care of her, son. Not sure I can fully trust a man who hates golf though." Her dad winked, and Jonah laughed.

"Sorry about that, sir," Jonah quipped.

Her dad winked and then took a spot next to her mom. Jonah took her hands, and the officiant stepped up.

"As this is a vow renewal, Jonah and Grace have opted to say their own vows. Grace?"

Grace nodded and pulled out a little piece of paper. "Jonah, when I first met you, I thought you were just this blond surfer from California, but you ended up being so much more. You were more than just my partner...you became my best friend. You gave me the legs to stand on, and I'm glad we ended up getting to know one another. I love you, and I'm proud to be your wife."

"Jonah?" The officiant gestured.

Jonah nodded. "Grace, when I first met you, you yelled at me about loading up the rig wrong and you refused to let me drive for weeks."

There was some laughter.

"I knew right then you were not the woman to mess with, but you were an amazing partner. The best to work with. Sorry, John," Jonah said over his shoulder.

"Not offended," John said, grinning.

"I love you, Grace. You reminded me that there is more to life. I was just existing and not living. You were very unexpected, but I'm glad that you're my wife and will continue to put up with me. I love you with my whole heart."

"I love you too," she whispered.

"You may both kiss and seal this vow renewal," the officiant said.

Grace stepped forward, and Jonah touched her face. "I love you."

"I love you too."

He kissed her gently, and she melted for him, just like she always did. There was clapping and they broke off the kiss, but she knew she wanted more of that later.

"I now pronounce you, again, Mr. and Mrs. Cute Paramedic."

Grace laughed, and Jonah just rolled his eyes as he took her arm and walked her down the aisle. Their family showered them with rose petals. She had her happily-ever-after months ago, but she was glad she was able to share this with her family.

And that Jonah was a part of her life. They were family. No longer alone.

Now and forever.

* * * * *

*If you enjoyed this story,
check out these other great reads
from Amy Ruttan*

Rebel Doctor's Boston Reunion
Tempted by the Single Dad Next Door
Reunited with Her Off-Limits Surgeon
Nurse's Pregnancy Surprise

All available now!

Get up to 4 Free Books!

We'll send you 2 free books from each series you try PLUS a free Mystery Gift.

Both the **Harlequin Presents** and **Harlequin Medical Romance** series feature exciting stories of passion and drama.

YES! Please send me 2 FREE novels from Harlequin Presents or Harlequin Medical Romance and my FREE gift (gift is worth about $10 retail). After receiving them, if I don't wish to receive any more books, I can return the shipping statement marked "cancel." If I don't cancel, I will receive 6 brand-new larger-print novels every month and be billed just $7.19 each in the U.S., or $7.99 each in Canada, or 4 brand-new Harlequin Medical Romance Larger-Print books every month and be billed just $7.19 each in the U.S. or $7.99 each in Canada, a savings of 20% off the cover price. It's quite a bargain! Shipping and handling is just 50¢ per book in the U.S. and $1.25 per book in Canada.* I understand that accepting the 2 free books and gift places me under no obligation to buy anything. I can always return a shipment and cancel at any time. The free books and gift are mine to keep no matter what I decide.

Choose one: ☐ **Harlequin Presents Larger-Print** (176/376 BPA G36Y)   ☐ **Harlequin Medical Romance** (171/371 BPA G36Y)   ☐ **Or Try Both!** (176/376 & 171/371 BPA G36Z)

Name (please print)

Address   Apt. #

City   State/Province   Zip/Postal Code

Email: Please check this box ☐ if you would like to receive newsletters and promotional emails from Harlequin Enterprises ULC and its affiliates. You can unsubscribe anytime.

Mail to the Harlequin Reader Service:
IN U.S.A.: P.O. Box 1341, Buffalo, NY 14240-8531
IN CANADA: P.O. Box 603, Fort Erie, Ontario L2A 5X3

Want to explore our other series or interested in ebooks? **Visit www.ReaderService.com or call 1-800-873-8635.**

---

*Terms and prices subject to change without notice. Prices do not include sales taxes, which will be charged (if applicable) based on your state or country of residence. Canadian residents will be charged applicable taxes. Offer not valid in Quebec. This offer is limited to one order per household. Books received may not be as shown. Not valid for current subscribers to the Harlequin Presents or Harlequin Medical Romance series. All orders subject to approval. Credit or debit balances in a customer's account(s) may be offset by any other outstanding balance owed by or to the customer. Please allow 4 to 6 weeks for delivery. Offer available while quantities last.

Your Privacy—Your information is being collected by Harlequin Enterprises ULC, operating as Harlequin Reader Service. For a complete summary of the information we collect, how we use this information and to whom it is disclosed, please visit our privacy notice located at https://corporate.harlequin.com/privacy-notice. Notice to California Residents – Under California law, you have specific rights to control and access your data. For more information on these rights and how to exercise them, visit https://corporate.harlequin.com/california-privacy. For additional information for residents of other U.S. states that provide their residents with certain rights with respect to personal data, visit https://corporate.harlequin.com/other-state-residents-privacy-rights/.